Although, Pat Graham loves being involved in theatre, he has always covered writing. This is his first real shot at getting a book published.

The other past writing experiences he has had are two poems published by United Press; also, he wrote the script for a musical, *Boy*, which was performed in the year of the holocaust and some silly poems about grandmas, written down in the first lockdown.

He hopes that the readers will find in *The Story of Jasper Gabalda and His Incredible Journey* something that they will enjoy reading.

For my daughter charlotte and my granddaughter Athena,
the two amazing people, who have followed their dreams.

Pat Graham

The Story of Jasper Gabalda and His Incredible Journey

Austin Macauley Publishers™
London • Cambridge • New York • Sharjah

A CIP catalogue record for this title is available from the British Library.

ISBN 9781398445734 (Paperback)
ISBN 9781398445741 (ePub e-book)

www.austinmacauley.com

First Published 2022
Austin Macauley Publishers Ltd®
1 Canada Square
Canary Wharf
London
E14 5AA

Thank you to Austin Macauley Publishers for helping me to become an author.

Synopsis

Jasper Gabalda is a smeldewok who helps the mothers of small disobedient children to get out of the bath, by putting his extraordinary long fingernail up through the plughole, to tickle the children's feet.

Once his work as a mother's helper is complete, Jasper with his friend Worminus is seeking to release his own world from the Time Zone, where an evil tyrant has placed it.

To succeed on this dangerous mission, the friends have to travel back to Jasper's homeland, involving them in battles with the dreaded meldoes who are trying to capture the pair.

On their journey, they receive help and protection from a mysterious being and a magical stone, enabling the friends to achieve everything they set out to do.

Chapter One
Introducing Jasper

It was a bright sunny day; the countryside looked beautiful, and as there were no clouds in the sky, you could see for miles.

A forest, overgrown with dense dark foliage, stood on top of a hill, and through the trees, a road could be seen winding its way down the hillside.

All that could be heard were birds calling to one another from their nests, until, a most unusual sound of something or someone humming a jolly tune filled the air.

Looking in the direction of the sound a black spot could be seen walking down the road, and as it walked, the afternoon sun cast a long shadow onto the spot, which turned the spot into a blob with arms and legs.

The nearer the blob came there were other things that you noticed.

In the blob's right hand, it carried a small brown case with 'MOTHER'S HELPER' and the initials J G printed on the lid in brass letters and looking, even more closely, you could see it wasn't a blob but a smeldewok.

For those of you who have never heard of 'Smeldewoks', they are a race of gentle, loving creatures who live in a world which is hidden in the depths of every Sewer Region under Planet Earth.

Here, they carry out their daily lives of caring and sharing, making their world a perfect place.

Smeldewoks are neither small, nor tall, have round bodies, extremely long arms and legs, but this smeldewok was different from all the rest…

Its head, which was a most unusual balloon shape, had two incredibly blue twinkling eyes.

Its hands had extra-long fingers and the index finger of its right hand had the longest nail ever seen.

All this belonged to Jasper Gabalda, the most beloved smeldewok of all times.

Many smeldewoks have to carry out their work on the earth plane, and as Jasper was one of the smeldewok who had to go to work, his job was to 'help the mothers of children who hated having to get out of a nice warm bath'.

The way that Jasper carried out this work was to put his long nail up the plughole, tickle the child's foot and hey presto, the child wondering what or who was tickling its foot would jump out of the bath, but before this could happen, Jasper had to find the bathroom he had to work from.

To help himself, he had 'A Magical Nose' which would wiggle, then twitch, and when the twitch turned into a sneeze, this was the signal to tell him that he had arrived at the place where he was needed.

But one day, something horrible happened in the Sewer Region.

An evil being called Madgoo the Grubber, who with his Army of Spies had arrived from the Dark Place, had taken over the Sewer Region and made rules which had to be obeyed.

Rule number one. FOR THOSE WHO WORK OUTSIDE THE SEWER REGION, A PLACE OF EMPLOYMENT HAS TO BE FOUND BEFORE THE SUN GOES DOWN.

And because of this rule, Jasper knew that the time had come for him to start out on his travels into the human world as soon as possible.

Picking up his case which held everything he needed for his work, Jasper started to walk up the long dark tunnel into the world above his own and not knowing when he would see his homeland again made a promise to himself.

"When I return back home, I will do everything in my power to destroy the Grubber and bring back peace to the Sewer Region." So, with these thoughts in his mind, Jasper set out on the most incredible journey of his life.

Chapter Two
Jasper Begins His Journey

After the long climb up the dark pipe into the human world, the sunlight dazzled in Jasper's eyes, and after waiting for a moment, Jasper saw to his amazement that everything looked ENORMOUSLY BIG...

Trees looked enormous, stonewalls looked enormous, everything he could see looked enormous, even the road in front of him seemed to stretch for miles and miles into the distance...

This is it, thought Jasper, *I had better find out where I will be working before the sun goes down or I will be in deep trouble.*

Starting to walk down the longest road he had ever walked on, Jasper decided to hum his little hum which would help him forget how tired he felt, but as he carried on walking and humming, things began to happen.

His magical nose began its twitch and wiggle which made him give the largest, loudest sneeze he had ever sneezed.

It was so loud that it shook the leaves off the trees, made birds fly out of their nests, and the people living in a nearby village thought they were having a massive thunderstorm, and as all this happened, he heard the words, "BLESS YOU!"

Jasper froze; where were the words coming from?

Looking around, the only thing that Jasper could see was a large brown wooden gate in the middle of a high stonewall, which was as wide as it was high, making it impossible for a tiny little being like himself to climb or to be able to see what was on the other side.

This was turning out to be quite a problem, and at this moment, Jasper had no time for problems; he just had to get where he was going, before the sun went down.

Thinking for a moment, a wonderful idea entered Jasper's brain.

If he could jump higher than the gate, he would be able to see what was on the other side, and because he was the highest and best jumper out of all his friends, this would be the answer.

Putting down his case, Jasper marched up to the gate, walked backwards and forwards in front of it and decided that ten-foot lengths would be just right for a good lift off.

After the ten-foot lengths, Jasper bent his long thin legs, did a hop skip and jump which propelled him high into the sky, and as he bounced along on a breeze, he looked down and there he could see below him, a gravel drive leading to a large grey stone house with three chimneys.

The walls of the house were covered in ivy. Honeysuckle grew around the green shiny front door and all the windows were sparkling in the summer sunshine.

At the front of the house was a large garden where, at the edge of the lawn, shaded by trees were two swings and a paddling pool.

Smiling to himself he thought, *Hurrah, this must be the place where I am needed because swings and paddling pools means children.*

Feeling very happy about everything, Jasper floated about, till all at once the air pulled him backwards making him land with a plop on the ground, and as he lay with his legs sticking up in the air, an awful thought came into his head.

I have found the place where I am going to work, but how am I going to get into the house? I can't climb over the gate with my little legs and a suitcase in my hand. Then, once again from out of nowhere came the words, "I will tell you."

Scrambling to his feet, he saw where the words were coming from.

From under the gate slithering towards him was a long green wormlike creature with an enormous head, two bright green eyes, two large nostrils but no mouth.

Chapter Three
The Creature

Jasper stood looking at the creature slithering towards him; then, he felt an itch in his leg, and looking to see what was causing the itch, he saw it was caused by the creature slithering up his leg.

Jasper knew the only thing to stop the horrible monster from climbing any higher was TO STICK HIS EXTRA LONG NAIL INTO ITS HEAD.

Letting go of his case, Jasper swung out his right hand and hit the creature, but as quickly as it fell towards the ground, the creature stretched itself up into one long tube and looked Jasper straight in the eye.

Staring back but not wanting the creature to know how frightened he was, Jasper pointed his nail at the monster, saying in a deep voice, "Slime ball, unwrap yourself from my legs or I'll slash you to ribbons."

Hearing these words from such a strange little creature with a loud menacing voice, the creature decided the best thing for him to do would be to move away as quickly as his long body would let him.

Giving a mighty flick of his tail, the creature dropped to the ground, slithered towards the gate, but just as quick, Jasper put out his right foot, trapped the end of the creature's tail, which made it fly through the air like a piece of elastic, bang its head with a big thwack against the gate to land, in a heap at Jasper's feet.

Pointing his long nail at the monster, Jasper moved around the strange creature till he heard, "Sorry so sorry, just curious, didn't mean to frighten you."

Quickly pulling back his finger, Jasper asked, "Did you speak?"

"Yes," hissed the creature.

Jasper couldn't believe that a creature without a mouth could speak through its nose, but having good manners, Jasper stopped looking at the amazing speaking nose and looked into the creature's bright yellow eyes saying, "You didn't frighten me; you startled me; guess, I'm a little shook up."

"So am I," the creature agreed looking back at Jasper, and as they both stared at each other, Jasper began to worry.

With everything which was happening, and how quickly time was spinning by, Jasper had to find a way over the gate into the house as quick as possible to start his work to avoid getting into trouble with the Grubber, so the best thing to do would be to get on with the job in hand.

As Jasper bent down to pick up his case and the creature began wriggling away, the sun disappeared behind a large black cloud, which made the pair say, "It's going to rain."

Looking at each other in astonishment, both asked, "How did we say the same words at the same time?"

"Single minds with but a single thought," said the creature. "But I've got to get inside, or I'm going to get wet."

"So have I," said Jasper, "but it's impossible."

"Why?"

"I'm too little, and the gate is too big."

Nodding his enormous head, the creature looked at the little smeldewok saying, "I can help you, but only if you tell me who you are and your reason for being here."

Chapter Four
Worminus and Jasper Tell Their Stories

"Why do you want to know about me?" Jasper asked.

"Because of my official capacity."

"Your official capacity?"

"I am Worminus Snak, keeper of this gate and have been since Roman times." Jasper gulped.

"That's a most unusual name, and if you don't mind me saying, you must be very old if you have been here such a long time."

The creature rippled its long body as it answered.

"Firstly, I was given the name because my mother was a worm and father was a snake; and yes, I am very old.

"Now, no more questions from you, only from me and my question is.

"What sort of a creature are you, because never in the whole of my existence have I seen anything like you."

Jasper began to feel cross; all he wanted to do was to tell the worm thing to shut his mouth, but how could he when the worm hadn't got one.

Once again, the worm hissed.

"Would you be so kind as to tell me what sort of a being you are and where you have come from?"

Being a nice sort of a creature, Jasper forgot about being cross and decided that the best thing to do would be to tell the creature everything about himself, so starting at the very beginning of his life, Jasper began to tell his story.

"I belong to a community of smeldewok, who live together peacefully in the Sewer Region beneath, the Drury Lane Theatre in London.

"I was born at the third sunrise during the beginning of the dark season and the reason I have been sent to the earth level is because of the work I do."

"You work?" the worm hissed.

"Doesn't everyone have to work, why do you ask?"

"Because here, only the long and tall work for the community."

"Where I come from, all smeldewoks who are healthy have to work."

"So, little creature, what do you manage to do in the great scheme of things?"

"I am a mother's helper for children who misbehave; I have a nose with a twitch, which is used for finding the place of my next job and a long fingernail used for tickling the foot of a child to make them get out of the bath when they don't want to."

Filled with amazement at the things he was hearing, Worminus became more so as Jasper carried on with his story.

"My homeland is now occupied, by the tyrant, Madgoo the Grubber, who invaded our region at the beginning of the third quarter separating all the smeldewoks into groups.

"The ones fit to work have been made slaves; the rest taken into captivity and sent to the Time Zone, which is a place, no one has ever seen, and from where, no one ever returns and also the Grubber has made rules that we all have to live by.

"One rule states that, 'All the smeldewok have to find and be in their new job on the Earth Plane before the sun goes down, or they will be returned to the Grubber, to work in darkness for the next twenty seasons."

Wanting to know more, the worm asked, "If this tyrant can't see you on the Earth Plane, how can he possibly know, that the rule hasn't been obeyed?"

"Because the Grubber has spies."

"What sort of spies?"

"They are evil batlike creatures called meldoe, who work above and below ground.

"Each meldoe has been given its own smeldewok to spy on, and it must never leave till the smeldewok either completes the mission, or fails."

"Where will your meldoe be?"

"We never know."

"So, what happens if you can't get to your new job?"

Looking very sorrowful, Jasper answered, "We are sent to the Time Zone or made to work with the teams who are building new pipe ways for the Networks travel system, which makes the Grubber very rich, because of the charges he makes for smeldewoks to travel through the Network."

How unfair, thought the Worm.

The little smeldewok looking very worried asked, "Please will you help me?"

Looking at his new friend, Worminus answered, “I most certainly will.” And because he wanted to make sure he could keep his new friend safe, things had to be started.

Immediately so, with the words ‘Follow me’, the task began.

Chapter Five
Getting Jasper over the Gate

Worminus slithered towards the gate then began to wiggle his tail towards the place where he wanted Jasper to stand while giving out the order, "Stand over here."

Jasper felt nervous, what was Worminus going to do with him?

"Go on, Jasper, do as I tell you," the order rang out.

Knees banging together, Jasper began shuffling along in a very silly way, making Worminus want to hiss with laughter, but at the same time, wouldn't, because he didn't want to upset his new friend.

Wiggling the end of his tail, Worminus shouted, "Go for it, Jasper; you are wasting valuable time, and there's not a lot of it."

Jasper shakily took up his position. "Well," hissed the worm, "is it yes, or is it no?"

Feeling a little bit ashamed of looking like cowardly custard, Jasper said all in one breath, "ALL RIGHT, I WILL DO IT."

Slithering towards Jasper, Worminus then rose into one long tube, split himself in half, wrapped his body around his new friend making Jasper feel as though he was stuck in the middle of Giant Green Jelly, and as he looked down at himself, Jasper saw that he had turned green.

All he wanted at this moment was to get out of Worminus's tummy, then something happened, and whatever it was, it was making him feel very frightened.

Jasper saw that they were beginning to move to the top of the gate, which was making him feel very funny, one minute he was looking up at the sky and the next looking down at his feet, then before he could think another thought, they had reached the top of the gate, and as Worminus flipped himself over, with a great rush of speed, they began sliding down the other side of the gate and as the movement stopped how happy he felt, till horrors of horrors, he found he could not move.

Opening his mouth, he shouted, "How do I get out?"

In answer to his question, Worminus filled his body with air, which made Jasper bounce around as though he was on a trampoline, and when he was full of air, he made his nose into one big hole and blew Jasper out saying, "There you are." As though this was an everyday happening.

Standing up on very shaky legs, Jasper said in an equally shaky voice, "That was the most amazing experience of my life."

Worminus, rippling back into his original shape, gave a big wink, saying, "No Problem."

The little smeldewok turned to his new companion asking, "How can I repay your kindness?"

Worminus turning his head, looked at Jasper, saying, "Don't repay, just stay."

To which, Jasper with a big grin on his face replied, "I most certainly will."

Chapter Six
In the Fir Tree

After their journey over the gate, the friends sat together on the grassy bank at the side of the gate; the only sound that could be heard was the rustling in the fir tree at the side of the gate made by a dark grey meldoe, an evil batlike creature belonging to the army of the Grubber who had been sent to spy on Jasper.

As the meldoe crouched on a branch of the fir tree, the rustling sound was made, as the meldoe turned on the box like receptor strapped to his side to record everything the smeldewok and worm said to each other.

The meldoe knew everything that was recorded would put the two friends in danger which would help him to become the right-hand winger, a prized position in the Grubber's Army.

Grinning evilly, the meldoe knew the rule. Number Two hundred and Nince.

'HELP FROM ANYBODY NOT INVOLVED IN JOB OR SITUATION WILL MEAN IMMEDIATE EXPULSION BACK TO THE REGION.' And how delighted he was that he had witnessed Jasper Gabalda being helped by a long green worm.

Unaware of what was happening, Jasper and Worminus carried on telling each other their stories, till they heard the rustle of pine needles, and as Worminus turned his enormous head towards the pine tree, the meldoe crouched down out of sight.

Jasper asked, "What can you see?"

"I? Nothing, but I thought I heard something."

"You must have a wonderful sense of hearing because I didn't hear anything."

"Little one, it's all down to vibrations."

Jasper put his head to one side.

"Vibrations, what are you on about, Worminus?"

"Well, my friend that is part of my story." And as Worminus began his story, the meldoe started the recording…

Chapter Seven
Worminus Starts His Journey

"I lived in Roman times, in the service of the centurion, Maximus Carnivio, where I was keeper of the gate; in fact, Jasper, the very gate we are standing in front of…"

Jasper looking at Worminus in amazement asked, "May I ask again how old you are?"

Worminus answered, "Ageless." Making Jasper feel slightly uncomfortable until he saw laughter in the eyes of his friend while Worminus gave a wink, asking, "May I continue?"

Jasper nodded.

"Okay then, no more interruptions."

No more interruptions, thought the meldoe. *Just get on with it*, as the receptor at his side carried on with its evil work of recording the big worm's words…

"The vibration test was my own idea. I would lay with my head on the ground to hear and feel vibrations of the approaching enemies, which kept my master and his family safe, and because of this idea, my master wanted to show how grateful he was by taking me to Rome, to receive the highest award, for dedication to one's work from Armild, the wisest being in the whole sphere.

"One morning, two soldiers came to where I slept carrying a beautiful casket of burnished gold with sides of mirrored glass; the inside was lined with red velvet and precious stones covered the casket's lid.

"As they gently laid me inside the casket, I was carried out to where my master stood with his guards at the front of the gate, and as we turned to wave goodbye to my master's family, we started out on the journey, which would change my life forever..." The meldoe's eyes gleamed with satisfaction; today was certainly turning out to be a good one and more so as Worminus continued.

"For many days, we travelled over land and sea, till we finally reached the shores of a land called Italy; here we travelled by vine-covered lowlands, crystal-clear lakes, till we came to the hardest part of the journey.

"Surrounding us as far as the eye could see were magnificent mountains, so tall that they seemed to reach up through the clouds, and the highest mountain was the one which would take us to our destination.

"Starting to climb the mountain, the paths narrowed, the air became colder, and just when we thought we would have to stop our journey, the sun broke through the clouds so that we could see miles and miles of towering mountaintops, coloured pink by the sun.

"After climbing for many hours, we finally reached the summit, whereas the sky darkened, millions of stars twinkled above us and my master's soldiers wrapped themselves in blankets to settle down for the night; as I lay, curled up in the comfort of the casket, looking out through its glass sides gazing at this magical sight until I fell into a dreamless sleep...

"Next morning as the sun began to rise high in the sky, the soldiers lifted up my casket for the journey down the side of the mountain where, as the paths became wider, the air warmer, we finally arrived at our destination, the Eternal City of Rome." Jasper gazed in wonder at his new friend and couldn't wait to hear the next part of Worminus's story, and up in the fir tree, the evil meldoe also couldn't wait.

Worminus began the next part of his story.

Chapter Eight
Rome

"Entering the City of Rome, we passed through squares filled with fountains of dancing waters, piazzas surrounded by magnificent buildings, long avenues bordered by graceful trees and everywhere the sound of bells could be heard making Rome a magical place.

"Finally, we arrived at a beautiful villa.

"The gardens were filled with brightly coloured flowers, wonderful trees and a marble terrace which led to a summerhouse where I would lay at my master's feet while servants brought food and drinks of honey nectar on golden plates and jewelled goblets.

"After a few days' rest, I was taken to a room which was built in a circle.

"Alcoves in the walls were filled with fountains of water, smelling like sea spray.

"The floor was the colour of the sea, and in the centre stood a long marble table on which the soldiers gently placed my casket, and as the soldiers left, two handmaidens, dressed in long flowing white dresses, entered the room…

"Lifting me out of the casket, they poured water over me from the mouths of gold fishes, polished me with oil, till I shone like a sunbeam and lastly sprayed me with beautiful perfume then as trumpets sounded, the soldiers entered the room, and I knew the time had come for me to meet the wise one…"

The meldoe began to feel uneasy because of the time the creature was taking to tell his story, and his time to report back to the Grubber, but he knew he had to gather what information he could, while Jasper couldn't wait to hear more about his new friend and so Worminus continued.

"Placed once more inside the casket, we journeyed on roads lined with cheering Romans till we arrived in a large square where in its centre stood a large white building carved out of white marble.

"Seven white steps lead up to a large door, surrounded by seven gold pillars, and there at the top of the steps was a magnificent throne, shaped like the body of a swan covered in a cloth of gold.

"In a toga of white linen, bejewelled sandals on his feet, his head adorned with gold laurels leaves sat the ruler Caesar Septimus who as he raised his hands a fanfare of trumpets rang out, and the Caesar spoke…

"'Today, my people, I have a duty to perform, which gives me great pleasure. I welcome to our great city, one who has never failed in his duty to others.'

"An ivory table was brought forward; my casket was gently lowered on to it as once again, Caesar Septimus spoke,

"'Good people, I show to you, Worminus Snak.'

"Cheer after cheer rang out as I was lifted out, and there in front of the people, Caesar Septimus turned to me saying,

"'The time has come, Worminus Snak, for you to meet Armild, the wise one', which, Jasper, was a meeting I will never forget."

And as Jasper smiled, so did the meldoe, who carrying on recording couldn't wait to hear the next part of the worm's story, which would be used to capture the pair.

Chapter Nine
Meeting Armild, the Wise One

"Caesar Septimus walked up the steps to the large carved wooden door, knocked three times, then, as if by magic, the door slowly opened, into the most magnificent room I had ever seen.

"The walls were lined with beautiful golden statues; crystal chandeliers shining like the colours of the rainbow hung from the ceiling and at the far side of the room, a door of pure gold, so tall, that it seemed to disappear through the ceiling could be seen.

"Moving towards it, we could see the door, had neither handles or doorbells, and as we wondered how we could open the door, something strange happened.

"Two golden platforms, on top of which stood two golden statues, rose up through the floor and like a musical box; as music played, the statues slowly moved around in a circle, reached out and pushed the door, which slowly opened into another amazing room.

"One wall of the room was made of mirrored glass; the ceiling, which was lit with thousands of silver stars looking as though they were floating on white clouds, was the colour of the sea; then as if by magic, a silver door appeared in the glass wall slowly opening into another mysterious room where the sound of tinkling bells could be heard.

"Entering this mysterious room, a soft mist rose and fell in gentle waves, and a silver curtain moving in a soft breeze opened for us to see, walking gracefully towards us, a slender being with long silver hair dressed in a long white robe carrying a small mother of pearl box.

"Speaking in gentle tones, the slender being spoke, 'I am Armild the wise one, welcome, o' Caesar, greetings to you Centurion.'

"'May I have the privilege of meeting Worminus Snak.'

"My casket was lowered onto a beautiful carved silver table, then as I was lifted out, Armild put the mother of pearl box by my side, stretched out his hands, and as he gently stroked my head, energy ran through my body making me feel as though a great force of power from some higher clime had entered inside me, and as I looked up into Armild's face, the kindness in his eyes moved me to tears.

"With a smile, Armild said, 'Worminus Snak, I can see for many seasons into the future, and you brave creature have been blest to live throughout eternity. I bestow upon you powers, to help all people and creatures who dwell above or below the ground, defending them from evil and harm. Finally, I bequeath into your care, this token.'

"Lifting up the mother of pearl box, Armild carefully opened the lid and there lying on a blue velvet cloth was a beautiful starshaped stone where from its star-shaped points, bright lights shone, filling every corner of the room.

"Picking up the stone, Armild began telling us of the mystery which surrounded it. 'This stone, the only one in existence, has lifegiving gifts, which can only be used when all is without hope, and you, Worminus Snak, have been chosen to be its guardian. I now place the stone into your safekeeping for the good of all beings for the rest of time, guard it well and wisely and all will be well.'

"Carefully returning the stone back into the box, the lid began to close, the lights dimmed, the stone disappeared from view and so did Armild, leaving nothing but the small mother of pearl box in the centre of the room."

Worminus turned to Jasper.

"Oh, Jasper, what a burden I have to carry, but whatever the cause, I will always fulfil all I have to do because of the trust placed in me.

"Whoever or whatever I help, I won't receive any thanks, because the thanks belong to Armild."

Jasper filled with love for this selfless creature knew whatever happened, he would never let this extraordinary being down.

The meldoe's eyes glistened, everything he had heard would provide him with the opportunity to put in force the one idea in his evil mind.

If he could get hold of this wondrous stone, it would help him to become the Grubber's right-hand winger, then he could overthrow his master and become ruler of the Sewer Region.

Chapter Ten
Travel Bags, Questions and Answers

Now that he had finished recording everything the worm had said, the meldoe turned off his receptor, gave a push against the branch of the fir tree to become airborne for the long flight back to the headquarters and the Grubber.

The rush of air from the meldoes take off, made Jasper and Worminus look upwards to see what they both thought was a bat flying across the evening sky…

"Oh, we must have frightened it," said Jasper.

"Never mind frightening bats," said Worminus. "Let's get you to your new plughole."

Worminus with long slithering movements moved towards the house, followed by the little smeldewok who with a funny skipping step tried to keep up then said, "My case, my case, it's on the other side of the gate."

"Can't it wait until daylight?" asked Worminus.

"No, it can't."

"Why?"

"Because there are things I need."

"Like what?" Worminus asked, wondering exactly what could be of such importance to the little creature standing at the side of him.

"It's my nail file."

"A nail file. Why do you need a nail file?"

"I need it to keep my nail in good nick."

"Doesn't he mind?"

"Doesn't who mind?" replied Jasper.

"Good Nick," said Worminus.

Jasper's mouth reached both ears as grinning broadly he announced, "It means, you are looking after things."

Feeling sorry for embarrassing his new friend, Jasper put Worminus at ease with, "No Sweat, Worminus."

The answer came back, "We never do."

"What?"

"Sweat, Snaks never sweat."

Jasper looked embarrassed while the eyes of the big worm twinkled with laughter but stopped as Jasper began speaking again.

"There is my Highly Technical Wet Suit Extraordinaire, known as a SWENTH, but in my case SWET, short for wetsuit."

"May I ask, what is a wetsuit?"

"I wear it when I am working."

Worminus blinked his yellow eyes in surprise…

"How can one work in something that is wet; it makes my skin crawl if I feel the slightest bit damp."

Jasper wanting to get into his new plughole before the sun disappeared knew he would have to give Worminus all the answers or else they would still be here for ages, so he began again.

"When I am working in a plughole and the water rushes down on me, if I didn't have a wetsuit to keep me dry, I would look like a drowned rat."

"Don't mention rats; you are making me hungry," said Worminus.

"You eat rats, but how do you eat rats when you haven't got a mouth?"

"We make our nose into one big hole and swallow it."

Jasper could not think of anything worse than having to put food up your nose, so quickly decided never to ask Worminus about his eating habits again.

"Sorry for making you feel hungry, but it was the only way I could describe the use of my wetsuit."

"Something wet keeps you dry, that's the funniest thing I have ever heard of." He then asked, "What is this remarkable suit made from?"

"It's made from the jelly that the jellyfish don't want."

"Really, how strange. I never thought those funny creatures were good for anything but dangling their legs in the water."

How Jasper wished Worminus would stop asking questions; the sky was beginning to lose the sunlight and this was beginning to worry him.

"But there is another question I would like to ask."

Oh, no, not again, thought Jasper, *if this is going to happen again and again, I've just got to say something.*

"Worminus, I am not being rude, but I really have to get where I am going before it gets dark, so could we please get question time over?"

"Sorry, Jasper," said Worminus but carried on with the next question. "If a wetsuit keeps your body dry, what about your head?" *Hobley Mobley*, thought Jasper, *here we go again.*

"It's a tight-fitting helmet which keeps the water out of my eyes."

"That's mighty clever," said the snake, which only had his own skin and not all these bits and pieces.

"But what is it made of?"

"Well, it looks and feels like—" Jasper suddenly stopped.

"What's wrong?"

"Can't tell you."

"Why not?"

"Because you won't like it."

"Why wouldn't I?"

"Because" – Jasper paused feeling lost for words then replied – "it's like a kind of snake skin." He quickly added, "But not quite."

"Better not be, my friend, because we are nearly all extinct."

Jasper looked down at his friend saying, "And I will be if I don't get my case, so if you can help me, I will be ever so grateful." Worminus lifted his enormous head from the ground, looked into the twinkling eyes of the little smeldewok, with the answer.

"My friend, I will always help, no need for thanks, don't repay, just stay."

Jasper humbly replied, "I will."

Dropping gracefully to the ground, Worminus began slithering to the gate while Jasper thought, *This is going to be mission impossible; how can Worminus get my case over the gate or even underneath it?*

And just when Jasper had given up hope of ever getting his case back, the worm turned his head. “Don’t worry; there are no problems, only solutions.”

Jasper’s mouth dropped open. “I never spoke.”

Back came the reply, “You don’t have to; it’s all down to thought transference.”

“You mean you know what’s going on in my head before I have even said one word?” The worm nodded.

Thinking for a moment, Jasper shouted, “You mean, you will be able to tell me to shut my mouth before I even open it?”

Worminus smiled as he moved under the gate thinking to himself, *We have so much to teach each other.*

Waiting for the impossible to happen, Jasper stood and watched as a rather fat Worminus flipped himself over the top of the gate, slid down, and as he reached the ground, a rumbling noise was heard, as Worminus joined his nostrils together into one big hole, gave a big blow, then, hey presto, out shot Jasper’s case.

Giving a wink, Worminus turned himself back into his usual shape hissing the words, “What a case he is!”

Jasper couldn’t believe that; he had just been thinking those very same words. He blurted out, “Am I never going to have any secret thoughts?”

“Only when I chose to tune in.”

Now more than ever, Jasper realised what a unique gifted creature Worminus was, not realising that one day this amazing gift of thought transference would help them to overcome the dangers they would face in the future.

Chapter Eleven
Jasper Finds His Home

Looking up at the sky, daylight was disappearing and time was moving on; the only thing that Worminus wanted was to get Jasper settled in his new home, so with a 'Come on, Jasper, let's get moving, pick up your case and follow me', they arrived in front of a drainpipe under the kitchen window.

Turning to Jasper, Worminus said, "This is the entrance, follow the pipe till you get to the place where you can rest. I will see you in the morrow when the sun rises."

With the words 'Have a peaceful night, my friend', Worminus happily slithered away to his den at the side of the gate, and for the first time, in a long while, Jasper felt happy; things were fine, and he had an amazing new friend.

Laying his case on the ground, Jasper set about getting the things he needed to help him find his way inside.

Opening the lid of his case, his ULTRA VIRAY ILLUMINATOR was the first object he came to; picking up the yellow tube-shaped torch, he pressed the green ball at the top, which made a pinpoint of light shine, out into the darkness, showing him that the inside of the pipe looked small, dark and narrow.

As he had to get on with his job, Jasper put his case under his arm and thought, *Here I go*. He bent his long legs and climbed inside.

Because he felt happy that he was inside the pipe, he wanted to hum, but humming meant the sound would echo around the pipes, which wouldn't be a good idea because, the people living in the house would hear the noise and want to know what was making it, so that meant NO HUMMING.

With the light shining from his UVI, Jasper could see in the distance that the pipe turned a corner. *Gosh*, he thought. *This pipe is longer than expected, anyway onwards and upwards till I get where I'm going.* And as he came to the bend and turned the corner, he saw that he was in the largest space he had ever seen inside any drainpipe.

Standing up, Jasper straightened his legs, dropped his case to the floor making the beam from the UVI shine around the space with a comforting glow, and looking around Jasper thought, *Wow, at last, a large space I can call home; this is great!*

Sitting on the floor, Jasper crossed his legs and saw a large iron nail sticking out of the wall. *Ha Ha*, he thought, *that will be a good place for hanging up my UVI with enough space underneath for my case, this is super-duper. I have a new job, a comfortable home, and the best thing of all, a new friend!*

For the first time for many seasons, he felt really happy, but being impatient, Jasper wanted to get everything ship shape before he started work.

Hanging his UVI on the nail, Jasper took out of his case, a small roll of shiny metallic material and a brown wooden tub with the name 'Stickle' printed on its lid.

Unrolling the material, Jasper laid it face down onto the floor, poked his long nail into the stickle and began spreading the sticky substance over the material.

When this was done, he turned the shiny side upwards, stuck it securely to the wall and as the light from his UVI shone onto the material, Jasper could see the image of a very handsome smeldewok staring back at him.

Gosh, he thought, *I can see me, what a good idea! I will call it an... 'I can see me'...*Feeling pleased for making something which would be very useful, Jasper felt life was good, but he hadn't finished yet.

Bending once more into his case, he searched around and pulled out a flat sticky-bottomed hook, and as he tapped the hook, it jumped out of his hand, turned itself into a clothes' peg and stuck itself to the wall.

Wow, thought Jasper, *this is great. I can hang up my UVI and put my jelly foot covers underneath.*

Feeling wonderful with himself that he was turning out to be an inventor of things, he went once more inside his case, and the next thing he pulled out was a little sheet made of bubbles; looking at it, for a moment, an idea came into his head.

Laying the sheet of bubbles on the ground, he folded it down the middle, stuck his finger into the stickle, stuck the edges together, turned it over and hey presto, there was a sleeping bag; now he had something to sleep in, which was another wonderful idea. Jasper then started to jump up and down on the sleeping bag to make sure that it had no lumps or bumps, and when he was happy that it was all straight and fluffy, he slipped his little body inside, pulled the top under his chin, let out a deep sigh, yawned, reached up his long thin arm to where his UVI hung, prodded it with his finger and turned off the light.

In the velvety darkness, he smiled to himself thinking, *Gosh, it's been a super day!* While at the side of the gate, one wormlike creature took a last look at the stars, scratched his tail on the end of a stone and curled up on his bed of pine needles.

Later that night, if you listened, you could hear sounds of musical snoring, while inside the house came the sound of voices.

"Can you hear that?"

"Hear what?"

"I'm sure there's a buzzing in the pipes."

"Well, whatever it is I'll sort it out in the morning."

"Listen, there it goes again."

"Shut up and go to sleep."

Jasper and Worminus oblivious to it all just snored and snored, unaware that in the sewer regions, the downfall of the little smeldewok and his friend was about to be plotted.

Chapter Twelve
The Meldoe's Journey

While the pair slept the meldoe turned towards the setting sun.

The news about Jasper Gabalda and his friend he was bringing to his Master Madgoo, the Grubber, would certainly make him the Grubber's right-hand meldoe, then he could start work on his wicked plan of getting rid of his evil master.

As he flew, his wings made a strong beating sound and the receptor strapped at his side bleeped, which was a signal from the trans-communication centre hidden in the depths of the Sewer Region.

Looking towards the horizon, he saw a bank of heavy cloud, and because the vapour from the clouds could cover the edges of his wings with a sticky substance which would make him lose speed and height, Meldoe 2 knew he must contact headquarters for the safest route to get him back to the Sewer Region.

Tuning into his receptor, the voice of Meldoe 4 became loud and clear.

"Meldoe 4, Meldoe 4 speaking. Meldoe 2, what is your message?"

"There is a large bank of cloud in my immediate flight path, give me instructions for a different route."

"Turn away from straight in front, go down, not up, continue straight on, arrive at the Sewer Region at NINETEEN FIVE O, not one cess later. Over and out."

Turning to his left-wing side as instructed, Meldoe 2 flew over the outer edge of the cloud bank, to continue on his journey, flying smoothly over valleys and hills, and as darkness fell, the lights shining upwards, from the human's homes below him, gave the world a magical appearance.

On and on, he flew till he saw on his right-wing side, the motorway, and as he followed the motorway's direction, he saw in the distance, the opening to the Dartford Tunnel, which is the entrance to the Sewer Region for all creatures from the underworld. Developing ridges on the edge of his wings to break his flight, he looked down for the best place to swoop towards the tunnel's entrance.

Looking towards the tunnel, Meldoe 2 saw something which would stop him entering the tunnel; it was a flight of gulls on his right-wing side, and the fear to a solo flyer of being surrounded by other birds was always a risk.

Meldoe 2 knew that, on his own, it would be impossible to fight the gulls, but he had to get back to his master.

Thinking about what would be the best way for him to attack, the idea came to him.

If he could fly beneath the gulls, he would not be seen; this would clear his way for entering the tunnel.

While he looked at the group of gulls he could see that the last gull in the group was the youngest; if he could take the little one hostage, that would be the answer.

Because of the rule, 'For all creatures that inhabit the skies, all young ones must come first', Meldoe 2 knew if the gulls saw the young fledgling wasn't following, they would break formation to look for the little one, which would leave him free to fly on his journey.

Shortening his wing ridges, he swooped forward, and as the beating from his wings caught the young chick's attention, the young one turned its head to see.

A mouth of large pointed teeth set in the face of an evil batlike creature.

As the chick called for his mother, Meldoe 2 swooped forward, captured the little one, and as the little chick's mother turned her head to see if all was well with her little one, she screamed, "NO CHICK!"

Using his wings and strength, Meldoe 2 disappeared from the gull's sight, dropped the little gull to the ground and carried on following the motorway, till the inside of the tunnel with the green light over the third drain cover came into view.

At last, he was near the entrance to the Sewer Region and the end of his journey.

Chapter Thirteen
The Dartford Tunnel

The third drain in the Dartford tunnel is the entrance from the human world into the Sewer Region, and the Grubber uses sqones, who he calls 'the lowest of the low', to open the drain cover for the returning meldoes…

Two little sqones, drab mouselike creatures, crouched together waiting for Meldoe 2 to arrive; they were so frightened that the draft from the racing traffic could drag them under the wheels of oncoming cars, but they knew.

If they left their post, they would be in terrible trouble.

Moving their little bodies against the wall to keep safe, they heard the sound of beating wings, which was the signal that the meldoe was near and time for them to start their work.

Moving forward, using all their strength, they pulled back the drain cover for the meldoe to make his landing.

Flying into the entrance, the meldoe brought his wings to his side, adjusted his receptor, carefully smoothed down his fur, knowing that once he had given his master the news which would bring about Jasper Gabalda's downfall, he would certainly receive the 'Order of the Underside, the Overseer of All Sewer Regions'.

With these thoughts in his mind, he pushed the two little sqones to one side and started his walk down the shaft to arrive at the Grubber's pod at the time ordered by his master.

The shaft, a tunnel which led downwards into the Sewer Region, was lit from the lights shining inside the Dartford Tunnel, but deeper under the ground the Shaft went, the Grubber had made inventions for his protection.

Placed in the walls were shiny eyes turning in all directions, used not only for lighting the passageways but for watching all that passed, with black clocks on the walls, turning around and around, each turn ticking out a cess to remind all smeldewoks 'TO BE LATE WAS A CRIME', while everywhere in the Sewer Region, the sound of NINCE NUNCE NINCE NUNCE was heard, made by the Bellow Pumpers pumping air through the tunnels.

As Meldoe 2 walked down the shaft, a group of sqones stopped work to let the meldoe pass but because the meldoe walked by without looking at them, which was most unusual.

The sqones knew that something must have happened, but not being able to stop their work, they must carry on, till they could get back to their quarters to discuss this most unusual event…

Hurrying down the dimly lit shaft, the eyes in the wall watched Meldoe 2 as he walked towards his master's cell, while, in the distance, three smeldewoks standing at the opening of corridor Wok, which led to their living quarters, stepped aside as the meldoe came nearer.

Bowing low to their captor, they asked, "Morrow, Morrow, Meldoe 2, how's Jasper, how goes it?"

Slapping his right wing against his side, he replied, "You will find out sooner than later, prepare his place again."

The smeldewoks looked at each other, something had gone wrong, and Jasper must be in deep trouble, which meant, all smeldewoks must be alerted to help their beloved friend.

Chapter Fourteen
The Grubber

Reaching the Grubber's cell, Meldoe 2 tapped on the black wood screen on which was carved the face of the Grubber and as the screen moved back, a voice rasped, "Enter."

Resting on a couch was the body of a large slug with a small head, which had eyes sunk in pools of fat and short stubby hands clasped across its enormous body.

This was the Grubber.

Surrounding him were tiny antlike creatures called anties, whose mouths made little clicking noises as they sucked out the dirt that nestled in the folds of his fat body, and as the Grubber shouted 'Away, away' to escape their fate of being squashed by the weight of this enormous being, the anties moved away, as quickly as possible.

A squishing sound was heard as the Grubber moved into a more comfortable position on his couch and looking down; he saw that one of the anties was still at work on his chest.

Lifting one sausage like finger, he flicked the little being through the air towards the serving sqone, who, on the order from the Grubber, put its foot over the defenceless little creature. Pointing at the meldoe, the Grubber said, "Tell me, tell me your news."

Moving towards the Grubber's couch, Meldoe 2 hoped that everything he had to say would bring him the position he wanted in the Grubber's army, as the Grubber, who always let his meldoes know that he was in charge, waited to see the meldoe squirm with fright, by letting the Black Clocks tick away the cesses before asking the next question.

Not knowing where to look, Meldoe 2 stood trembling, as the Grubber waited a few more cesses then shouted, "What rule has been broken?"

"Your latest one, master."

Pointing a finger at the attending sqone, the Grubber rasped the order.

"Fetch me the keeper of the Book of Rules NOW!"

Not daring to disobey, the sqone scuttled out of the cell, as the Grubber stared evilly at Meldoe 2 saying, "I hope you have some good news for me."

Meldoe 2 could feel his wings start to tremble; if he did not complete the task, it would mean elimination from duties, then, his plan to bring Jasper to the Sewer Region would never happen.

Another tap on the screen turned the Grubber's gaze away from the trembling meldoe, and on the command 'Enter', the screen once more opened to reveal the sqone and a smeldewok who was holding the Book of Rules.

Bowing low to the Grubber, who sat drumming his fat fingers impatiently on the edge of the couch, the little creatures moved forward as the command was rasped out.

"Show me the book; show me the book."

Gazing with hate at their captor, the Keeper of the Book lifted up the enormous Book of Rules.

Chapter Fifteen
The Rule Book or What Is Known as a Book of Rules

The Book of Rules was a most unusual shape; it was twice as long as it was wide; the cover looked and felt like dried mud; the first page was at the back while the reading went from the end of the book to the beginning; in fact, a most unusual work of art.

"Now," snapped the Grubber, "find me the rule about what, Meldoe 2, about what?"

Meldoe 2 gulped nervously.

"Yes," said the Grubber drumming his fingers on his great belly, "what is the rule?"

"About not being helped," was the answer.

A feeling of dread filled the cell, as the Grubber motioned the Keeper of the Book forward asking, "Was Smeldewok Gabalda aware of the rule?"

Feeling sick with worry but wanting to keep Jasper safe, the smeldewok knew he would have to agree with the Grubber. He answered, "The rule was made before Jasper left the Sewer Region."

Again, the question was asked, "Was Jasper Gabalda aware of the rule?"

Even though the smeldewok knew that Jasper didn't know about the rule, he dropped his gentle head and nodded to agree with his evil master, how he hated himself.

Pointing at the attending sqone, the Grubber rasped, "Find me the rule which proves Jasper Gabalda has done wrong and set the black clocks for 400 cesses."

Turning towards the Keeper of the Book, the Grubber commanded, "Smeldewok, if you cannot complete the task in the 400 cesses, you will be sent to the Time Zone."

Quickly flicking from page to page trying to think which part of the book the rule belonged to, the words 'Not to be helped' kept going around in the smeldewok's head; he could not remember seeing the rule then a thought came into his mind.

"Every season, the Grubber sets a test stating that all rules have to be remembered. If I can't remember seeing the rule, it must be a new one."

Excitedly, the smeldewok turned to the back page and there it was, Rule Two HUNDRED and NINCE.

The smeldewok looked up from the book.

"Yes, yes," rasped the Grubber.

"It is the Rule Two hundred and Nince, which states, 'No smeldewok shall accept or ask for help'."

There was silence in the cell until the Grubber commanded the sqone to stop the Black Clocks, then, as everyone waited for a burst of anger from the Grubber, the Grubber smiled and said, "Congratulations, the rule Two hundred and Nince is correct, as you have completed the task within the set time, you may go back to your quarters." And as the smeldewok closed the book, the Grubber with an evil leer gave out the chilling command 'Tell no one' while giving the thumbs down sign, which meant exterminate.

Clutching the book to his little body, the smeldewok walked backwards, as was the order for anyone taking their leave of the Grubber; all he wanted was to get back to his quarters, assemble the others and devise a plan that would keep Jasper from harm.

Chapter Sixteen
Meldoe 2 Tells All

Once, the keeper of the Book of Rules had left the chamber, the Grubber turned to Meldoe 2 ordering him, "Tell me, word for word, all that you have witnessed." And so, the meldoe began.

"Smeldewok Gabalda arrived safely at his place of work, where an obstacle of a large gate stopped Smeldewok Gabalda getting into his place of employment, then from under this gate, a wormlike snake appeared, wrapped Smeldewok Gabalda inside its body and transported him over the gate."

A look of interest appeared on the face of the Grubber as he shouted in a high-pitched shriek, "Carry on, carry on!"

"Master, a conversation between the worm and Smeldewok Gabalda took place about strange and wonderful things and one of these is a special stone, with lifegiving properties."

Excitedly, the Grubber pointed a fat finger at the meldoe, shrieking, "Meldoe 2, who holds this wondrous stone?"

"The worm, my master."

The Grubber rasped out, "Set the Black Clocks for 300 hundred cesses, which is the time allowed for you to tell me about the creature."

On the Grubber's order, a sqone kneeling, in the darkest corner of the cell, jumped up, ran over to the Black Clocks pushing the middle of each one; the clocks started the countdown.

With a tremble in his voice, Meldoe 2 once more repeated the story, making sure that every fact was in place and, after listening intently, the Grubber screeched out.

"I must have this stone; then with all its power, I will rule the sphere forever. Stop the clocks." And as the clocks were stopped, the Grubber beckoned the meldoe to his side. "You have done well, Meldoe 2; you must now make a plan to capture Smeldewok Gabalda and his friend.

"Take as many meldoes as you need for the operation, and on completion of the task, your reward will be a place on the Sornod."

With the evil thoughts of 'if everything turns out in my favour, I will overthrow you' in the meldoe's head, he humbly bowed to his master, who ordered, "Bring me the plan by the morrow."

On these words, Meldoe 2 left the Grubber's cell, turned in the direction of the Sentinel to make his plan, which he hoped would give him a place on the Sornod, the council of the mighty, then, who knows, what might be next.

Chapter Seventeen
The Battle Plans

Walking down the corridor towards the Sentinel where each meldoe has its own private pod, a gang of sqones who were cleaning the eyes stopped in their task to bow to Meldoe 2, who thinking only about his plan walked past them without looking, and as he neared his pod, he sent out three sharp blasts from his personal calling device to tell his sqone he was on his way, and when his master appeared, the little sqone bowed low and opened the door.

Entering the pod, the meldoe pushed the little creature to one side, making the sqone know he was in for a hard time. How he hated his master…

Inside the pod, the eyes on the walls lit up the pod, a stone table stood in the centre and, in the darkest corner, a wooden bench with a kneeling pad for the sqone was placed against the wall.

Slapping his wings to get the sqone's attention, the meldoe ordered, "Bring me writing materials."

Going over to a dark square chest placed in one of the alcoves, the sqone lifted up the lid, brought out parchment and a scrawling stick, placed them in the middle of the large stone table, pulled up a bench, and when everything was ready, the meldoe walked over, aimed a swift kick at the little creature, spread out the writing materials, to begin making plans to capture Jasper and bring him back to the Sewer Region. As Meldoe 2 carried on writing, he found that his ideas for the battle plans were coming thick and fast.

First, he would allow himself a squadron of sixty meldoes in six groups of ten, to fly in the opposite direction from which he had travelled back to the Sewer Region.

Flying the squadron of sixty out of the tunnel would not be an easy task but the easiest way to solve the problem would be for all meldoes at regular intervals to fly out in pairs, linking up at the edge of the forest, by the side of the motorway.

All personnel would need ultra-narrow sharpened bites with covers for their teeth, and each group leader would be issued with receptor detectors, and the start time for Operation Capture Gabalda would be dusk.

Now that his plan was taking shape, Meldoe 2 could start plotting the route to capture the smeldewok, the worm and the all-important stone.

Putting down the scrawler, he shouted, "Time for blip blops. I need to feast!"

Scuttling towards a copper pot near the door to where a wooden ladle hung, the little sqone picked up the ladle, lifted the top off the pot, scooped three ladles of blip blops into a large oval dish, carried the food over to the table making sure that he did not spill one blip blop…

Because he was so hungry, he wished the meldoe would leave him one of the blip blops, but as usual, the meldoe greedily pushed them all into his mouth till the dish was empty, which made the little sqone hate the Grubber, his henchmen and the occupation of his homeland even more…

Working through the night till the battle plans were ready, the meldoe stretched his wings then called out, "I will have fifty cesses relaxation before I see the master."

The downtrodden little sqone pulled out a bed from a space high in the wall, stood back as his master lay down to rest, and after the turning Black Clocks had counted the fiftieth cess, he stopped the clocks, stretched out his hand and gently touched the sleeping meldoe.

Meldoe 2 sat up, rubbed his eyes, stretched his grey fur body, beckoned his sqone to pull back the bedsheets and when this was done, stepped down from his sleeping space, raised his wing and once again pushed the little sqone to the floor.

As the little helpless creature lay where he had fallen, the meldoe picked up the battle plans and left the room, ready for his appointment with the Grubber.

Chapter Eighteen
The Battle Plan Is Revealed

Reaching the Grubber's pod, a sqone opened the screen while the Grubber, lifting his head from where he lay on his couch, looked, evilly in the meldoe's direction rasping, "Come forward, Meldoe 2; let me see what is planned for the return of Smeldewok Gabalda and this Worminus Snak."

Running to get the bench, a sqone, placed it by the table, waiting for the meldoe to sit, and when this was done, on the rasping order of the Grubber's 'faster, faster', the meldoe quickly unrolled the parchment scroll, and as the plan was revealed, the piggy eyes of the Grubber burnt with greed then he gave out the order of, "Gather all meldoes together, leave at the end of the morrow. Remember, you must not fail. I will eagerly await your return with the captives and the stone."

Rising to his feet, Meldoe 2 looked at the Grubber, thinking, *One day, I'll be sat where you are, then I will have rendered you down, to nothing but a container of fatty oily gung.*

He walked backwards as was the Grubber's order, while, from his corner, the little sqone who had listened intently to the evil mtosome's conversation couldn't wait till he was safely back in his Ezze to inform his comrades about the plan to capture Jasper.

Standing at the end of Corridor Wok, the two smeldewoks watched Meldoe 2 hurrying back to the Sentinel, both knowing that something must have happened, and because the eyes in the corridor had been dimmed for cleaning purposes, they knew that they could talk more easily…

"He didn't notice us, so he must have something on his mind," said one of them. "If we knew what is happening between the Grubber and his spies, we might have a chance to help whoever is in trouble; we must call the others."

The couple hurried down Corridor Wok to their Ezze and, once inside, called an assembly.

Tapping out a rhythm on the pipes messaging system, which had been invented by Jasper's father, immediately the Ezze was filled with creatures, knowing that something important must have happened.

Once the entrance was closed, two sqones went to get the prodders, 'discs on sticks', used for turning the eyes in the walls in different directions, so that they couldn't be spied on by them, and once this was done, they all sat silently in a ring.

The first smeldewok spoke, "There's a mysterious urgency about Meldoe 2, who never saw us standing at the end of our corridor; he just walked quickly by…"

The little creatures, worry etched on their kindly faces, looked at each other knowing this was a most unusual happening.

Another of the group asked, "What do you think it's about?"

"I can tell you," said the keeper of the Book of Rules, "I know that Jasper Gabalda is in trouble."

"Why?" asked one from the back.

"It is something about Jasper breaking one of the rules."

"Why do you say that?" exclaimed another.

The Keeper of the Book moved to the centre of the floor then began to tell them out everything he knew…

Chapter Nineteen
The Smeldewoks Make Plans for Jasper

"Friends, I was called today to take the Book of Rules to the Grubber, and the task the Grubber set me was to find the rule that states, 'No one must receive help to complete a task', and according to the testimony of Meldoe 2, Jasper has been helped."

"Who by?" asked one of them.

"By a very large creature."

One after the other, the crowd started raising their voices, till one smeldewok loudly shouted, "This rule must have been written after Jasper left for his assignment or else Jasper would have known about it."

"That's just the kind of sneaky thing the Grubber would do" – one little smeldewok sighed – "and Jasper will be found guilty even though he doesn't know anything about the rule."

Another voice said, "Did you hear what the Grubber was going to do about it?" Turning to look at the assembled crowd, the Keeper of the Book shook his head, saying, "I was sent away and told to keep my mouth shut."

The hub of voices became louder.

"Hush," said one of the elders, "if we are to help Jasper, we must keep quiet; any sort of trouble could cause all of us to be sent to the Time Zone."

"Sorry," muttered one of the sqones, "but it makes us so angry that Jasper is in trouble for doing something he is unaware of." The elder of the group spoke out.

"We need to find out the Grubber's plans because if we can't solve these problems, we will never be able to help."

Silence fell till a question came from the back of the crowd.

"Which of us knows anything about the trimetric system? The reason I ask is because I want to know if it would be possible to rig the trimetric system in such a way, that we could overhear what is going on in other areas of the Sentinel and beyond."

"I am a trimetrician," replied one of the smeldewok, "and I will give thought to the matter. It may be possible to sort it out before anything happens to Jasper, and if I can do this, it will be one step nearer to helping all of us on our path to freedom."

Starting the work to help Jasper, the trimetician's workplace was filled with a curious crowd of smeldewok and sqones; all watching the trimetrician work steadily for many cesses looking into the back of the all-seeing eyes.

Holding up one of the eyes which resembled a round hard ball, the trimetrician explained, "One small hollow tube into the back of the ball will not interfere with the vision, while the front of the eye is the area where I will need help from everyone. I need a messenger, sending to the sqones who keep the region clean to save all tubing and coils, which have been left from the sweepings, so that the smithsons can make these into implants which will be used for making sound travel through the eyes."

"I'm a Smithson," said a smeldewok at the front.

Another spoke, "I'm a messenger."

The trimetrician looked around at the assembled company, then spoke, "Smeldewok and sqones, with everybody's help, we will succeed with this operation." All voices shouted together 'We will' knowing that one day their beloved friend Jasper Gabalda would once more be safely back in their midst.

Chapter Twenty
More Plans

Inside the Grubber's pod, a sqone, who was finishing his duties, exchanged the Grubber's notes with his replacement TZ 10, glad that his day in service to the Grubber was over.

Arriving at his Ezze, as he pushed the partition covering the entrance to one side, he heard voices. Waiting for a cess, he stepped nervously inside, to find the Ezze was filled with his comrades. Feeling frightened, he asked, "What's wrong?"

"It isn't good," TZ 45 replied closing the door as two of the sqones went to shut down the illuminators, and when all was quiet, he told them about the meldoe's plan, for 60 meldoes to fly out of the region to the place where Jasper Gabalda is working and bring him back to the region.

TZ 3 spoke up, "Why are they doing this? Jasper has never been in trouble for doing his work, and he has never been a troublemaker."

"There must be something else," said another.

"Yes, there is," said the sqone. "Jasper has had help from some sort of creature."

The cry went up from the assembled sqones. "Is this a crime?"

The sqone lifted his hand.

"According to the rule two hundred and nince, 'To be helped is not allowed', which was brought into force after Jasper had left for his work."

Meldoe 2 said, "Jasper had broken this rule, which means, when Jasper is captured, he will be banished to the Time Zone forever."

Again, came the cry, "How can he have broken the rule if he didn't know about it?" Each creature felt helpless; they all hated the Grubber, and now it appeared, he was going to take their beloved and trusted friend away from them forever.

While they were wondering what they could do, the sound of footsteps was heard in the corridor; had someone heard them plotting? Quietly, "Twenty, twenty four zero was said," as TZ 45 ordered.

"Let the smeldewok in."

Chapter Twenty-One
Putting Plans in Place

Going to the partition, two sqones opened it as quickly as they could, gave a sharp tug, then pulled the smeldewok inside, and as the smeldewok pushed his way to the front, the worried creatures crowded around him asking, "Smeldewok, what brings you here; you will put yourself and us in great danger if you have been followed."

The smeldewok replied, "I have made sure that I wasn't followed, but I have had to come to tell you that, something bad is going to happen."

The sqone, who had just arrived back from his duties with the Grubber, pushed forward; he wanted to tell the smeldewok what he knew and so he began.

"While doing my tasks I heard that Jasper is to be hunted down and brought back to face the Grubber; so, we must all work together for Jasper's safety." And as the voices within the Ezze started getting louder, the smeldewok lifted his hand to silence the crowd, aware that every creature was troubled as himself, while all the little creatures wanted to do was to tell the smeldewok about their plan of getting information from the Sentinel by using the eyes to see and hear everything in the region, as they told the smeldewok of the plan.

"How can this help Jasper?" was his question.

TZ 45 replied, "If we use the idea about the eyes, we can hear what plans the Grubber has made for Jasper's capture."

Then the smeldewok put forward his idea. "As, most of the meldoes will be absent from the region when they leave to capture Jasper, this will clear the way for us to attempt an uprising."

"What about the Grubber?" asked the sqone.

The smeldewok smiled. "He won't be closely guarded because nearly all the spy force would have left."

Joy was beating in the heart of every creature; here was something which could release them from the tyranny of the Grubber. Silence fell as TZ 45 addressed the assembly, "Everyone must unite in this task to save Jasper," knowing in his heart, that the entire Sewer Region would carry out the plan to help their beloved Jasper and restore their magical world back to peace and harmony.

Chapter Twenty-Two
Jasper Starts His New Job

Unaware of what was happening in the Sewer Region, Jasper stirred in his sleeping pouch.

Opening one eye at a time, he looked around but couldn't see anything familiar.

Where am I? he thought and then remembered exactly what had happened before he went to sleep. New plughole, new job, new little beanie.

(Beanie in smeldewok language is the name for a small human being.)

Stretching out his body, he scratched the top of his head, opened the edge of his resting pouch, stuck out his legs and walked over to his 'I can see me'.

Looking at himself, his smiley face looked back. *Nice face*, he thought, pulling his mouth into a big smile till it touched both ears, stuck out his tongue as far as it would go, pulled it back and decided, *I really must clean my teeth.*

Flicking open his case with his big toe, he bent down, found his toothbrush; next, he brought out a tube of Toothpoof, pierced a hole in the top of the tube, which made a small cloud of powder smelling of bilberries settle on his toothbrush.

Stretching his mouth even wider, Jasper started brushing his teeth while at the same time humming loudly, which is a rather clever thing to do, because one can't hum and brush one's teeth at the same time, and when he was satisfied that he had an ultra-gleaming smile, with great gusto blew the powder out of his mouth.

Now that he was clean and shiny, all he wanted to do was to get on with the task in hand so, standing in a military fashion, bent, touched his toes, stretched his hands above his head, ran on the spot, jumped up and down a few times, declared himself fit and ready to explore his new surroundings…

Turning out of his space into the gloomy shadowy pipe way, Jasper started following every turn, till, in the distance, a glow could be seen, and as he got nearer, he could see that the glow was a light shining through, A BATHROOM PLUG.

This was the place where he was needed…

Hurrying along, his long legs walked quicker and quicker till he was at last peering up through the plughole of a beautiful pink bath.

Bending himself in half, he put his foot against the side of the drainpipe, looked up and saw, above the rim of the bath, a room filled with shiny white tiles.

Blue and pink towels were placed on a shelf above the bath and around the bath's edge, bottles filled with coloured liquids stood in neat lines, giving Jasper the clue that, both kinds of beanies lived here, but the question Jasper had in his mind was, *What kind of beanie will I be working with and when will I start my job?*

The words 'Come on, Amy, I will not call you again', answered all of Jasper's questions of finding the beanie who would not get out of the bath, the words carried on coming.

"I've had a bath," said Amy.

"No, you haven't; that was yesterday."

"Well, if I get in, I won't get out." Knowing a battle was about to start in this bathroom, Jasper realised:

'THE JOB STARTS NOW.'

Not expecting things to start so suddenly, Jasper noticed that, he hadn't any work clothes with him; this was the most stupid thing he had ever done; the answer was that he would have to get back to his space as quickly as he could...

From his doubled in two positions in the pipe, Jasper moved his body into his usual shape, then, with the grace of an athlete, his thin legs moving like pistons, ran back down the pipe to his living space.

Flicking the switch of his UVI, to light up the room, Jasper went to his clothes' peg, pulled down his SWENTH, laid it on the floor, wiggled about, till his little body was inside, then, he reached up for his helmet, lifting it off the hook, stretched the sides and popped it on his head.

Laying down his jelly covers, side by side, Jasper bent his knees, propelled himself upwards and landed feet first inside them, then walked over to his case, punched his abacus inside the lid, to record the time for the start of his job.

Chapter Twenty-Three
Magic Messages

Humming softly to himself, Jasper started up the pipe till he saw something he had not noticed before, in front of him was another pipe going in the opposite direction.

Jasper stopped.

"Did I go to the right, or did I go to the left?"

As if by magic, a message came into his mind.

"Go to the right; if you don't, you will be going in the wrong direction; there is only right and wrong."

Jasper was amazed; the only creature who could have sent him such a message must have been Worminus, and if a smeldewok could be gobsmacked with this new-fangled Tele-Communication of receiving messages, Jasper was but deciding to give this new way a try. Jasper sent out this message, "Worminus, with being nowhere near me and guiding me in the right direction, this makes you a genius."

The message was sent back. "It's all down to thought transference, my friend."

Wow, thought Jasper, *what a great mate Worminus is.* Directed by Worminus's thoughts, Jasper turned to the right and carried on following the pipe, then all at once, for some unknown reason, he couldn't see anything at all; something had happened.

It was as if something had switched the light off.

All at once, he realised it was because, the bath plug had been put in and that he had forgotten to bring his UVI, which meant, he had to go back to his space again…Running back down the pipe as fast as his jelly foot covers would let him, he reached his space, climbed inside, picked up his UVI, turned on its beam, ran back for the second time to the plughole then, puffing and panting with all the extra running he had done, reached the plug, sat down, crossed his legs and waited for his job to begin as voices were heard from the bathroom.

"Amy, into the bath."

"No, I am not getting in."

"Young lady, I am going to get very cross."

"I'll put some bubble bath in for you."

"No, please," he wanted to shout, "bubbles sting my eyes, and I'm going to need my boggles. I really should have thought about everything I needed, what a crocky wocky I am."

The race began again, long spindly legs running like the wind and once inside his space Jasper went to his case to look for the boggles.

No boggles! Where were they; what was he going to do if he couldn't find them? All of a sudden, he felt a sharp pain in his toe and looking down saw laying on the floor, sticking into his big toe, the boggles, which must have fallen out of his case. Picking them up, he placed them over his eyes and as quickly as possible went back to the plughole, arriving just in time to hear the bath filling with water.

Chapter Twenty-Four
The Plughole

Standing in the pipe, not only could Jasper feel the warmth from the bath but he also could hear Amy splashing about; this was the moment he had been waiting for, because he could now start to collect those all important points for tasks achieved, and just as he waited for the next step, he heard the all-important words he wanted to hear.

"Out you come, young lady."

"Please, Mummy, don't pull the plug out."

"First, you don't want to get in, now you don't want to get out, well, young lady, I will make your mind up for you."

Adjusting his boggles, Jasper pulled his helmet to fit his head, pointed the finger with the magic nail upwards in readiness for the plug to be pulled out, and as this happened, the darkness in the plug turned to brightness and a trickle of warm scented water began to fall, followed by a rather fierce gush, which fell fast and furious on to his helmet.

Putting his lips together, Jasper blew into the water making a large multi-coloured bubble appear, and as popping bubbles with his finger was a game he loved, he carried blowing and popping till he heard Amy say, "Mummy, please put the plug back."

"No, Amy, you are coming out, or you will have to stay there till you feel cold."

"I don't care," wailed Amy. "I'm staying here."

Jasper looked up through the plughole where he could see a little fat foot; now was the time to start work.

Pushing the all-important finger up through one of the holes, he positioned his nail right in the middle of Amy's big toe and started to tickle.

Amy screamed.

"Mummy, Mummy, get me out; there is something tickling my foot!"

"Don't be silly, Amy."

"But there is. Mummy, please get me out of the bath!"

With these words, Amy's feet disappeared, leaving Jasper saying, "Hubbly Bubbly, nice work."

Wrapped in a large warm towel, a shocked Amy pleaded, "Please, Mummy, look down the plughole; there's something down there."

"Don't be silly; how can anything be down inside the plug?"

"Well, there is."

"If there is something down there, then I must say a very big thank you to it for making you get out of the bath so quickly."

"Please look down into the plug, Mummy."

"All right, darling."

As Amy's mother looked down into the plug saying,

'thank you very much', Jasper whispered back, "You're welcome."

"Did you hear that?" shouted Amy. "I thought I heard a thank you."

"Don't be silly, Amy."

"Well, I did and that's that." And immediately, she jumped off her mother's knee, looked down the plug to see a smiling Jasper looking up at her.

The pair stared at each other.

Amy now knew there was something inside the plug, which could speak. She shouted very loudly, "Mummy, Mummy, come and look; there's a creature looking up the plug."

Jasper flattened himself against the pipe, and as Amy's mother looked down, Jasper disappeared, making one mummy say 'don't be so silly' while one little girl knew that she wasn't.

Chapter Twenty-Five
Jasper Meets a Beetle

Task completed, Jasper shone his UVI around the pipe to make sure that all was well, then something happened.

From out of nowhere, two glowing lights appeared throwing out a powerful beam of brightness, which dazzled his eyes while at that very same moment, from the darkest corner of the pipe, a voice whined, "You are invading my space."

Jasper then saw.

Almost as black as its surroundings, a large scarab beetle with two long antennae sticking out from each side of its head; it fixed its glowing eyes on Jasper with an evil stare then whined, "If you do not leave my place, I shall do battle because, intruders must not intrude."

Jasper answered back, "I am not intruding; I'm working for my living."

Moving its hard shell-like body into a menacing position, pincers lowered, the beetle emitted a high electronic noise, and as the noise became louder, Jasper was so glad that his tight-fitting helmet blocked out some of the sound but knew he was now facing grave danger so the best thing he could do was to use his long nail…

Holding his nail out towards the horrid creepy crawler, Jasper gave out the command, "If you take one step towards me, I will slash you to pieces."

The scarab beetle, for the first time, was amazed that, his electronic sound had not brought the intruder down to his knees and was even more amazed that the intruder showed no sense of fear, but he was the one who now had to show the creature who was boss.

Once again, he raised the electronic sound, and once more, Jasper pointed the nail into the beetle's line of vision, saying, "Stop making that terrible noise or I shall pierce your shell."

Waiting for a second, the beetle looked craftily at Jasper then with a most incredible movement, shot its antennae forward, but just as quick, Jasper jumped into the air, landed on top of the antennae tipping the beetle sideways.

With jelly from his shoes, Jasper spread a sticky substance over the beetle, then told the beetle, "Either you get back to your corner and let me get on with my job, or I'll leave you here to rot. What is it to be, retreat or remain in a sticky position for the rest of your life?"

The scarab whined, "I'll let you carry on."

Jasper, wiggling his nail in front of the beetle, gave out the order, "I will be coming here once a day, and if you do not leave me in peace to carry out my work, I shall stick and stab you, so scuttle off, to your hidey hole..."

Dipping his head, the beetle rubbed his antennae on the floor to remove the jelly, and as Jasper shouted 'COCOON', the beetle scurried off into the blackness without giving a backward glance in Jasper's direction.

Jasper couldn't believe what had just happened; no matter how happy and content he felt, he now knew that he must always be on his guard against any trouble which might come his way.

What a day it had been, getting lost, a stand-up argument with a hideous scarab beetle, all he wanted at this moment was his resting pouch, and the quicker he got there, the better.

Entering his space, Jasper put the UVI on its hook, and as it hung there, its beam sent out a warm glow making the space look cosy and homely.

Hanging up his clothes, Jasper scratched his little round tummy, unzipped his jelly envelope, jumped inside then reaching out turned off the UVI.

As the space was filled with velvety darkness, Jasper feeling very sleepy settled down in his jelly cover sleeping bag till he heard the message. "Good night my friend, you have done well, see you tomorrow."

Jasper sent his thoughts winging back to his friend.

"Good night, Worminus, and thanks for all your help."

While in its slimy living quarters the beetle thought to itself, *Nothing will take over my territory, and once I have got my antenna into the creature, it will keep me in food for a very long time.*

And as it lay in the damp and darkness, the beetle began making plans to remove Jasper from his domain.

Chapter Twenty-Six
Silly Sayings and All That

An unusual noise made Jasper stir in his sleep; then, as the noise came again, Jasper really woke up.

"What's that rattling noise?"

The noise rattled again.

Jasper sat bolt upright thinking, *Oh dear, it's an eruption, the earth will start shaking.*

In answer to the question, the message came, "There hasn't been an eruption, silly little creature; it's me who's making the rattling noise."

"Gosh, Worminus, then you must be a 'RATTLE SNAKE'."

"If I'm a rattle snake, then you Jasper are CHINESE."

"How can I be Chinese?"

"Well, Chinese use woks and you are a smeldeWOK."

While they laughed at each other's jokes Worminus thought he had better explain what had happened.

"Jasper, I shook the pipe with my thoughts, not my body. I wanted to make you get out of whatever it is you sleep in and do whatever it is you have to do when you wake up, because, my friend, we have a lot to talk about."

Now bright-eyed and fully awake, Jasper slid out from the warmth of his jelly cover, sending back the message.

"I'll do my toiletrees, eat my blip blops then I'll be out."

"What are blip blops?"

"It's my food for the day; I have one when I get up."

"What do they taste like?"

"Sweet bubbles that go blip blop while melting in your mouth, very refreshing and stimulating."

"I wish I had blip blops instead of boring old flies; I could do with something to tickle my tastebuds."

"I will be out in about a hundred cesses, and I will bring you one to try."

"How long is a cess?"

"As long as you want it to be."

"Okay then, I'll be waiting by the gate, at the entrance to my pit. It's a beautiful sunny morning so we will be able to sunbathe as we chat."

Jasper took a blip blop out of the blip blop tin, enjoyed every mouthful, then brushed his teeth, zipped up his jelly envelope, looked around; he was so pleased that everything was comfortable and that he had a new friend.

Leaving his space, he walked down the gloomy pipe, till the sunlight lit up the entrance and when he reached the opening, jumped to the ground, took a deep breath of the pine scented air and walked over to meet his new friend.

Holding out his hand, Jasper said, "Good morrow, Worminus."

And as he opened his fingers, Worminus stared in fascination at a little red and white striped ball, and on the order of 'Open your whatever it is, and I'll drop in a blip blop', Worminus began joining his nostrils together, and as a hole appeared, Jasper dropped in the blip blop, which made Worminus give a very loud burp making him say, "Sorry about that, think I'll stick to flies in future."

"Thank goodness for that," Jasper added. "Because I don't want to try a fly."

Once they had got the blip blop thing out of the way, the pair sat together in the sunshine as Worminus asked, "How went it?"

"Worminus, it was scary; in the blackest corner of the pipe, there lives a scarab type beetle who makes threats to remove me from its domain."

Turning his head while giving a hissing sound, Worminus looked anxiously at Jasper saying, "Scarab did you say?" Jasper nodded. "Then, I'll have to enquire into this matter. Scarab is Egyptian, which means the creature is ancient."

A cess of silence fell between them, till Jasper said excitedly, "If it lives in the pipe, it won't be able to stand any light."

"You've got it in one," hissed Worminus.

"Any more trouble, Jasper, use the UVI, that will give it the Tombmees Kamoonees."

"Tombmees Kamoonees, what's that?"

"Well, beanies say Ebee Geebees, I say Reptilius Senilius."

Thinking for a moment, Jasper grinned delightedly.

"Ooh, I say Hubbly Bubbly, because it's to do with my job, bubbles and all that."

"Tombmees Kamoonees for Beetles. You're right, Jasper, Hubbly Bubbly for because, I want to be a wide-awake snake I always say Reptilius Senilius."

All of a sudden, the sound of a door being opened interrupted the pair.

Worminus hissed, “Quick get into my pit.”

And as the pair disappeared into the open entrance, they looked out to see two pairs of feet, one big, one small, walking past, as one little voice said, “Don’t forget some plasters; I’ve got a scratch on my big toe.”

“I won’t,” the other said.

Jasper grinned as the feet disappeared then turned to Worminus with, “Hubbly Bubbly, Worminus, that could have been ‘Double Trouble’.”

“Now you’ve got it; it’s all about silly sayings.”

“You are wise, Wormy my friend. I learn something new from you every day and Tombmee Kamoonee will certainly learn his lesson tonight.”

“Goody Buddy,” hissed Worminus.

Turning his head, Worminus saw that the humans had disappeared, so with ‘Coast clear’, both friends settled down in the glorious sunshine.

Worminus asked, “Please tell me about all about yourself.”

“How long have you got?” Jasper asked.

“As long as twenty of us put tail to tail.”

“Okay, that should do it.”

And when they both stopped laughing about their silly conversation, Jasper began his story.

Chapter Twenty-Seven
Jasper Tells His Story

"My father came from Italy and that is where I was born."

"Something in common, Jasper my friend, I went there to receive my award."

Jasper stopped telling his story as Worminus looked at his friend with a 'please carry on'.

Back came the answer. "That's what I'm trying to do, stop interrupting."

"Sorry, so sorry, just—"

Jasper finished the sentence with, "Curious! Just keep quiet, Worminus, so that I can continue."

Feeling silly, Worminus vowed he would never ever interrupt again, so for the third time, Jasper began his story.

"My father was part of the Gabalda family, the eldest wokling in a family of six living in the Sewer Region of Naples."

"What's a wokling?" Worminus asked.

"A wokling is a small smeldewok."

Worminus opened his eyes wide. "Oh, I get it, like a snaklet."

Nodding in agreement at the big worm, Jasper said in a stern voice, “You’ve done it again, Wormy, shut up, keep your nose closed.”

“I will, my friend, I will.” Jasper once again for the fourth time continued his story.

“My father came from a musical family who played the epanola.”

Worminus lifted his head to speak, but Jasper quickly said, “The epanola is a beautiful instrument which makes magical music, but my father didn’t need to play music on the epanola because he made wonderful sounds with his voice.”

Worminus was grew more and more enthralled as Jasper carried on.

“One day, Grandfather Stronie gathered the family around him to make an important announcement, ‘Tenora, which is my father’s name, the time has come for you to go to London to meet the Impresario, Granpo Onkle, who will give you singing lessons to make you into a wonderful singer.’

“With this news, my father’s case was packed for him to begin his new life, and Father started out on his travels to London to work with Granpo Onkle, whose habitat was beneath the world-renowned Drury Lane Theatre. Father kissed and hugged Grandma, waved to his friends and started out on the journey, which would one day make him world famous and where he would meet the love of his life.”

“I suppose that’s where you came into the story.”

“That’s right,” said Jasper, “but—”

“I know, SHUT UP!” said Worminus.

“For many cesses, Father travelled the Network, helped on his journey by kindly smeldewoks till, at last, he reached the Sewer Region of London.

"Asking directions to the theatre, it was always the same reply, 'You must be looking for Granpo Onkle; go down Drury Lane to the third pipe way on the right and there you will find the theatre.'

"As Father followed the instructions, he found the theatre, and once inside the wonderful building came across a dimly lit passageway, and as he walked along the passageway, he could hear in the distance, music.

"The nearer he got to the sound, he then found himself in a rather large room, and there moving towards him with tiny little skipping steps was a very flamboyant smeldewok, who announced rather grandly.

"'Welcome to this seat of musical excellence. My name is Arthur, ART because of what goes on in here and HI-JR, for whatever you can think of, and in the scheme of things, my job is to welcome and take all new students to meet the Impresario, so Signor Gabalda, please follow me.'

"Arthur skipped along very quickly, which made it difficult for my father to keep up with the funny little creature, and after traveling for quite some time through lots of pipe ways, they eventually came to another large room.

"Standing in the centre of the room was a large epanola, a magnificent musical instrument made of ebony, which shone like a polished black jewel, and there, dwarfed by the size of this grand object, on a high stool sat a very tiny smeldewok. The tiny little smeldewok while still playing wonderful music said, 'Thank you, Arthur, you may go.' And as Arthur skipped away, my father who was left standing alone, in front of this very important being, felt very nervous as still facing the epanola, the little smeldewok said, 'I am Granpo Onkle' then added, 'Welcome to Drury Lane, Signor Gabalda, I hope you are going to become as good as your father makes out, because I can't do with time wasters. You start in the morrow, so be prompt and punctual.'

"As the lid of the epanola closed, Granpo Onkle called for Arthur with the order, 'Take Signor Gabalda to his space, and I will see you, Tenora, no later than cess 50 on the morrow.'

"And with this, Granpo Onkle disappeared so quickly that my father had no idea in which direction he went."

Worminus was amazed. "Gosh is there more?" he asked.

"Yes, a lot more."

"Oh, do carry on."

"I will, if you stop interrupting."

"Only curious," was the reply.

"The next day, Father started his work with the Great Impresario singing scales, phrases and learning songs from great operas, and after many cesses of study and work, the Impresario announced, 'It is time for you to sing with another smeldewok.'

"In the twinkling of an eye, standing before my father was the most beautiful graceful creature he had ever seen, who holding out her hand said, 'I am so pleased that we are going to work together.'

"That, Worminus, was the beginning of a most wonderful friendship between my father and Aspra Ginelli…"

"And I suppose that is where you come in," added Worminus.

Jasper just smiled and continued with his story.

Chapter Twenty-Eight
The Story Continues

"Every season, there is a time when the theatre is not in use, which beanies call 'The Dark Time'."

Worminus looking at Jasper, opened his nostrils to which, Jasper stuck his long finger in the air, wiggled it about as he said the words.

"Beanies are humans and the dark time is when the theatre is closed for care and repair, which becomes 'our time to use the beautiful theatre' so no more."

"I know." Worminus sighed. "No interruptions."

Jasper carried on.

"Smeldewoks came from far and wide to the theatre where they would sit enraptured, as on the stage, the tiny figure of Granpo Onkle would play beautiful music to accompanying the voices of my parents…"

Worminus was enthralled. "It must have been a wonderful happening."

"It really was," said Jasper, "but it became even more wonderful when King Cuthbert, the kind ruler of the Sewer Region, was so impressed with the talents of my parents, that, he immediately made my father, the Minister of Song."

"Because of this important position, Mother decided to give up her life on the stage and assist Father in his duties and that is where I came in.

"One day, they went to the bubble room; this, Worminus, is a room filled with mud bubbles where, inside each bubble, lives a tiny little wokling, and when they finally decided which was the right bubble for them, that was when they picked me.

"Oh, Wormy, I had such a wonderful time as a wokling; my life was filled with love, music, performers and theatre; it was magical.

"As I grew older, what I wanted to do was to help woklings and beanies, by giving back all the love I had received."

Worminus smiled as only a worm could smile at Jasper's words and waited to hear the next part.

Jasper began, "Life was wonderful until—" then stopped.

"Until what?" questioned an anxious Worminus.

"The uprising."

"What's that?" asked Worminus, and this time, Jasper didn't stop him but carried on.

"The uprising was when the Grubber and his army invaded the region taking us all into captivity."

Worminus stared sadly at his little friend while Jasper carried on.

"I have made a vow that when I have finished my work with Amy, I will return to my homeland, destroy the Grubber and restore the region back to the king."

Worminus hissed, "Remember Armild and his prophecy?" Jasper nodded to overcome to speak as Worminus added, "Now is the time to show you the stone."

Slithering into his home, Worminus came back carrying a casket in his nose, laid it on the ground and touched the lid as it slowly opened.

There, lying on blue velvet, was the stone.

Jasper could not stop looking at the stone as Worminus whispered, "This stone is the answer to all our problems; it will help us if ever we find ourselves in trouble, and with its help, we will get back to the Sewer Regions."

Worminus then gently touched the casket; the lid slowly closed, leaving the stone hidden from view, and as the sun started to go down, Worminus slowly stretched his long body, saying, "You'd better be getting back to your space, my friend, work to be done."

Giving a smile, Jasper stood up, saying, "Thank you for today; it's been hubbly bubbly."

"Sure has," said Worminus. "But don't forget your light tonight."

"I won't." And with that, Jasper walked towards the house, turned, gave a wave as Worminus picked up the casket.

Slithering into his pit, Worminus sent a message to Jasper via thought transference. "Together, we are in this forever." Which was the worm's way of letting Jasper know that he would never be alone in his fight for right…

Jasper felt happy; at last, he had found a true friend who would help him restore peace back to the region.

Chapter Twenty-Nine
Back to Work

Filled with a wonderful feeling, Jasper climbed into the drainpipe remembering, 'Always go to the right.' And with these thoughts in his mind, he climbed through the darkness of the drainpipe, knowing that soon he would start out with his new friend on their journey back to his homeland where he would save his fellow smeldewok from captivity and the evil clutches of the Grubber.

Before this could happen, he knew he had to carry on with the tasks he had been given, so the first thing Jasper did, when he arrived back into his space, was to get everything ready for his job and have supper before he started work with Amy.

Sitting down, Jasper crossed his long thin legs, popped a blip blop into his mouth, and as the delicious taste of his meal filled every corner of his tummy, he folded his hands across his little body, then noticed, his remarkable nail needed attention, so with a 'I must sharpen it' reached over to his case, rummaged inside, pulled out his nail file, pointed his index finger in front of him, making sure the nail was in the right position and started the process.

Backwards and forwards, the file went till his magical nail was fit and ready for the job then, the next thing was to exercise.

Jasper started jumping up and down, flexing and stretching as a big smile stretched from ear to ear, how he loved it, then he started to hum out of sheer happiness, and as he jumped higher, each hum got louder till, Worminus sent Jasper a message.

"Stop it, Jasper, I can hear you out here."

"Okay, Worminus, will do." Which made the worm smile, thinking what friends they had become and what friends they would remain.

After wriggling into his SWENTH, Jasper jumped into his foot covers, peered at himself in the shiny material on the wall, but instead of spending time admiring himself, he knew he had better start work; so, after putting on his helmet, Jasper picked up his boggles and started walking towards the bend leading through the tunnel to the bathroom plug then came the message.

"Your light, Jasper."

"Gosh my UVI, thank you, Worminus."

Again, came thoughts from Worminus.

"Haven't you forgotten something else, little friend?"

"What?"

"Your A B C."

"My abacus, gosh, Wormy, what would I do without you!" And as Jasper picked up and primed his abacus, the message came.

"Go for it, Jasper my lad."

The answer was sent back, "I most certainly will."

Walking along in the darkness of the pipe, Jasper could see in the distance, the light shining from the bathroom plughole. *Nearly there*, he thought, and as he reached the plug, he settled down to wait for the time to start work, and what he wished for started to happen.

As the plug was put in place, it went dark inside the pipe, but Jasper could hear what was being said in the bathroom.

"Amy, please get in the bath, but don't play around too long in the water or it will get cold." And as the water swished around, Jasper knew that Amy who was enjoying her bath would certainly not get out.

"Stop playing about, just get out immediately," was heard…

"All right, Mummy, I'm coming."

"When?"

"In a minute."

"Now I am mean now." And as the words were said, suddenly there was brightness as the plug was pulled out. *This is it*, thought Jasper, *I must start my work.*

Putting his finger with the magic nail up the plughole, Jasper touched one little fat pink toe and carried on tickling till.

"Mummy, something scratched my toe, please get me out. I don't know what it is, but I don't like it, and I promise I will never stay in the bath again."

Jasper smiled and as he was about to move away, took one last look up to the plughole, just as a voice from above laughed.

"Your imaginary friend in the plughole certainly needs thanking, so whoever it is, Thank you very much."

"Mummy, you don't believe me, do you?"

And to prove that she was right, Amy peered down into the plug to see Jasper looking at her wiggling his finger.

Amy stared in amazement, shrieking, "Mummy, Mummy, there is something down there, and it's got a long finger!"

"What imagination you've got, just come along."

"No, there is, take a look."

As Amy's mother's big brown eye looked down through the hole, Jasper flattened himself against the pipe, so that he couldn't be seen while Amy shouted, "Is it still there?"

Her mother replied, "All right, Amy, whatever it was, it has gone, but just think, you will have a plughole friend every bath time."

"I don't want a plughole friend because I will never stop in the bath again."

Jasper smiled thinking, *Good bye, Amy, good job, well done over and out.*

Then, the light was turned out, the bathroom darkened, and the bathroom door closed. Jasper sighed.

"Bye-bye, Amy, I could have been your friend but can't stop, because I have important work to do."

Then something happened.

Chapter Thirty
Jasper Is Captured

As he started back to his space, Jasper shone his UVI into the darkness, and then found he couldn't move; there in front of him was a wall of stickiness.

Putting one foot forward to try to make a hole in the horrible stickiness, Jasper found himself sticking to the floor and could see that the scarab beetle was moving towards him. With a piercing electronic screech, the beetle gave out the message, "I told you not to come to my domain." Jasper knew he had to do something.

Pointing his UVI in the direction of the whining voice, the beam of light stopped the scarab beetle in its tracks as Jasper saw, from the end of its antennae, the beetle shout out a sticky black solution, which was covering his UVI, leaving them both in murky blackness.

Once again, the scarab whined out a message.

"The rules I live by were made centuries ago, at the ancient Pyramids, in the land of the Pharaohs and because of the powers given to me, you cannot escape.

"I will now entomb you, then, I WILL EAT YOU!"

Jasper felt helpless, the stickiness the beetle was shooting out was now up to his chest; his SWENTH was clinging to his body and as the beetle continued spurting, all that could be seen of Jasper was the top of his helmet.

With his pinchers, the beetle kept rolling Jasper over and over till he was wrapped in a mesh-like container of black gung, as he screeched, "I shall leave you to start crystallising and then my feast can begin."

The beetle started moving away into the blackness; its hard shell-like body scraped across the floor then, there was nothing but silence.

A large tear rolled down Jasper's cheek as he thought, *What am I going to do? If only Worminus could help me.*

Something in his sleep disturbed Worminus, making him open one eye then, closed it again thinking, *It's still night, the stars are shining, better go back to sleep.*

Again, Worminus stirred. *What is it that is disturbing me?* And once again as he opened his eyes, he could hear a faint voice saying, "Terrible trouble."

It came again. "Terrible trouble."

This time, the sound became clearer as he heard.

"In terrible trouble."

Worminus was now completely awake and straight away sent out the message.

"Jasper, is that you?"

"Yes."

"Where are you?"

"I'm just below the bathroom plughole; I've been imprisoned by the scarab; he's encased me in a sticky solution of black threads. My feet are stuck together, and I'm going through a process of crystallising so that the beetle can feed off me. Please, Worminus, help me before it is too late."

Worminus felt an overwhelming fear; he must not fail in the mission to save his friend; now was the time for the stone to be used.

Slithering over to where the casket was kept, Worminus picked up a disc-shaped object filled with blue oil, laid it at the side of the casket and after blowing open the top of the disc, lifted it up very carefully with the end of his tail, bent himself in two, poured the oil over his body to make it easier for going through drainpipes, opened the casket, picked up the magical stone, pressed it into one of his nostrils and started to slither out of his den across to the drain.

Because his body was so long, Worminus found it hard to push through the opening of the pipe but once inside slithered as quickly as he could, and the only thing which was worrying him was that, if the water came down the pipe, it would wash off the oil of his body then, he would not be able to move forward. But he had to carry on.

Worminus pushed along the dark twisting pipe till he reached the bend then, sent out the message. "I am on my way."

Back came the reply, "Please hurry because I am solidifying."

"Where's the beetle?"

"I don't know; all I can hear is a distant whine."

Worminus pushed his body as fast as he could through the pipe to where his friend was entombed, as the beetle waited in the darkness.

Chapter Thirty-One
Saving Jasper

In the silence of his den, the beetle heard a noise; he had to be on guard because he was a scarab beetle of the Royal Dynasty and no one should ever intrude into his domain.

Standing in battle stance, antennae stretched out in front of him, he started his terrible electronic screeching sound, and as the sound carried down the pipe, it made Worminus stop, his nostril tightening around the stone.

Staying as still as he could, he looked along the pipe and saw moving slowly towards him, two protruding antennae and as the beetle came into view, Worminus propelled him forward, ready for the next move.

Turning himself around, he gave the scarab a mighty thwack with the end of his tail, which sent it flying up the pipe, then blowing hard, down the nostril which wasn't carrying the stone, blew the scarab into the wall, breaking off one of its antennae then, looked down at the insect, hissing.

"Whose mercy are you at now, you horrible scarab? You believe you can harm anyone or anything, well, you are wrong; this place is no more your domain than any other creature."

The whining stopped; Worminus carried on.

"You think you have the right to destroy everything which crosses your path, but your master will not be pleased that you have turned yourself into an unscrupulous creature, defiling all that is good." And as the beetle started to whine and scuttle away, Worminus turned into the bend in the pipe, knowing the scarab would have to wait till his antennae had grown back before he could fight again.

He sent out the message, "Jasper, where are you?" There was no reply.

Again, Worminus sent out the message, "Jasper, where are you?"

Still there was nothing.

Worminus quickly began to push himself forward because, he knew he must be near the place where Jasper lay; then as he moved forward, he found that he couldn't move forwards or backwards; it was as though his body was laid in something sticky, then, in a flash, he realised that the stickiness had come from the beetle's antennae, so that meant he must be near to the place where Jasper was entombed.

Looking into the gloom, Worminus could see something which looked like a large cocoon, and although he knew he was still in danger, he slithered towards it, raised his head and looked inside, then he saw.

Jasper wrapped in black goo…

Worminus was horrified; for the first time in his existence, he didn't know what to do. He could not bear to lose the best friend he had ever had, and as tears sprang from the brilliant green eyes, the big worm realised it might be too late to save his friend.

Feeling nothing but sadness, Worminus felt that he had failed to save his best friend and that there was nothing more he could do. Then, from out of the darkness, a voice spoke to him.

"I gave you power many seasons ago, to help all those in adversity, do you, Worminus Snak, doubt my words?"

Raising his head, Worminus saw a blue light surrounding the cocoon, where appearing through the rays, a tall slim figure could be seen…

"Armild, is that you?"

"Yes, Worminus, it is, use your power."

"Oh, Armild, I don't know how to!"

"Try, Worminus, try!"

Looking at the chrysalis, his mind working hard, Worminus sent his gift of thought transference inside the cocoon and the heat from this amazing energy slowly started to melt the strands, and even though this was happening, Worminus still couldn't bear the thought that Jasper might never wake up.

Once again, Armild spoke.

"Why do you despair, Worminus, you have the power to restore life."

Worminus looked anxiously towards the misty figure of Armild, who raising his hands said the words, "The stone, Worminus, the stone." And as Worminus blew down his nostril, the stone fell onto the ground, and Armild disappeared from sight…

Pushing it with his head, Worminus moved the stone, till one of its points faced the cocoon, and as the stone began to glow, the light became so bright, lighting up the dark surroundings of the scarab's den; the stickiness started to melt. Worminus placed the stone in Jasper's hand, and as

Jasper's gentle eyes opened and with a sob in his voice, Jasper said, "Thank you, Worminus, thank you."

"Don't thank me, Jasper, thank Armild."

As the last strands of black gung melted, Jasper was set free from the terrible cocoon; now all Worminus had to do was to get his friend away from this terrible place as quickly as possible.

With great care, Worminus placed his large head under Jasper's body, pushed him into an upright position and Jasper tried to stand up, on a pair of very wobbly legs. "I don't think you are going to manage, are you?" said Worminus. "So I will do the obvious."

Once again, Worminus split in two, wrapped himself around the little smeldewok and the pair started to move away from this terrible place, leaving behind the scarab in its dark dingy den.

Worminus felt very tired, but down through the pipe, they travelled, till they arrived at the opening, and once in the fresh air, Worminus blew Jasper, who was still holding on to the precious stone, out through his nostrils; then together, they moved into the safety of Worminus's pit.

Once they were safely inside, Worminus lifted the stone carefully out of Jasper's hand, opened the lid of the casket, placed the stone inside.

Jasper asked, "How can I ever repay you, my wonderful friend?"

The reply came, "Don't repay, just stay. Sleep now for on the morrow, we must begin our journey back to your home."

Curling up with Jasper, Worminus was ready to shield him from harm and adversity, which they would both have to face on the most momentous of journeys they would ever have to make.

Chapter Thirty-Two
The Plan Takes Place

In the darkness of the approaching night, sixty evil meldoes assembled together in a wooded area at the side of the motorway waiting for the command to start their mission, and on the command, 'Sharpened bites at the ready', the meldoes knew that their mission to capture Jasper Gabalda had begun.

Each meldoe took from the opening of their receptors a pair of sharpened bites, which they placed them in their mouths, and the command came from Meldoe 4.

"To complete the task of capturing Smeldewok Gabalda and his companion, Meldoe 20, 22, 31 and 34 will be responsible for carrying the Ultra Narrow Opening Covers, all personnel will follow the motorways until the morning light. Turn towards the left-wing side, avoid all cloud formations, synchronise your guiders to face northwards and tune in your receptors.

"Start your journey now. I will be in constant command."

On Meldoe 4's order, Meldoes 20 and 21 picked up the long tubes of closely woven net, placed them in their mouths, while 31 and 34 made sure these were fixed securely by two clasps then, with a whooshing sound the platoon took off on their evil journey. Smiling, Meldoe 4 knew if he could succeed with this mission, the network would be his, making him 'Ruler forever'.

While the platoon became airborne Meldoe 4 became more assertive.

"Meldoes 35 to 50, once you have flown over the forest, keep us in your sights; your frequency receptors must be ready." And as the whine of receptors being put into action could be heard and the first set of meldoes could be seen in the sky, the rest started out on their mission.

Flying, with strong beating wings, each receptor was tuned in and on the command 'Upwards', the platoon flew slightly higher.

As the platoon flew on, the receptor of Meldoe 4 bleeped, and a voice was heard over the airways.

"Meldoe 2 reporting; Meldoe 2 reporting. Here is your weather check…Northern flying areas are clear. Your flight path is good. Report back to the Grubber in the next 1000 cesses, over and out."

Meldoe 4 surveyed the batlike creatures flying together; he would keep the platoon on track till their mission was completed.

At last, the journey to capture Jasper Gabalda had begun…

While in the Sewer Region, the smeldewoks were on first time alert; the trimetrician's clever plan of using the eyes to listen had worked, making every smeldewok aware of the plans to capture Jasper, and now, if the worse came to the worse, they also had a plan to catch the Grubber.

Chapter Thirty-Three
Jasper and Worminus Begin Their Journey

As the meldoes began their journey, Jasper and Worminus stirred on the comfy bed of pine needles inside Worminus's pit…

Raising his large head, Worminus looked at Jasper asking, "How are you feeling?"

"Hubbly bubbly," Jasper answered as Worminus unwrapped himself from around the little smeldewok, who after stretching one leg and then the other, lifted his hands, wiggled his fingers and when all was working well, thought, *I'm in fine shape.*

A soft breeze blew into the pit, and the wonderful smell of nature made Jasper's nose wrinkle in delight, then a large tear rolled down his cheek, which fell on the end of the worm's tail…

"What's wrong, Jasper," Worminus asked adding, "don't cry, you are alive and free; there are no problems, only solutions, and the only thing we must do is welcome the challenge we both face of getting you back home, so let us make preparations for our journey."

Jasper pulled his face into a thinking position.

"Are we travelling light or shall we be able to carry my case and things?"

"No, definitely not," said Worminus. "All that you brought with you the first time was for your work experience; this, Jasper, is going to be another experience."

"But can I take my blip blops and my UVI, oh, then there's my jelly envelope."

Worminus shook his head.

"I'll be your jelly envelope; you can sleep on me so just get your blip blops, and then let me see how big your UVI is before I decide about that.

"First things first, Jasper, back to your space pick up what I suggested; the sooner we start the better."

Jasper stood up, his legs feeling a little shaky as he walked towards the drainpipe; reaching the opening, he doubled up and climbed inside as his legs began to feel stronger, then starting the walk to his space, Jasper started thinking.

I've only been here for a short time, but what a lot has happened.

I did a good job with Amy, met the terrible beetle and what a wonderful friend I have in Worminus.

A message came from Worminus.

"If you don't get a move on, we won't be able to start our journey."

"Sorry," said Jasper as the reply came back. "Just get a move on."

Once inside his space, Jasper looked around for his UVI and remembered, *I left it by the bathroom plug, which solves a problem, because I can't get it.*

Back came the reply, "That's solved one problem so come on…"

Bending down into his case, Jasper found a season's supply of blip blops in a small container. But he shrieked, "How am I going to carry them?"

"Just bring them out and I will deal with it."

Jasper looked around his pit for the last time thinking about the time he helped Amy, but now that was over; it was time for Worminus and himself to get back to the Sewer Region.

Clutching his blip blops tin, Jasper moved down the pipe, and as he climbed out, Worminus was waiting for him while hissing, "I was getting rather worried about you, but true to form, Jasper, you always make it, so let's hope we make the rest of it."

"We will, you'll see."

Unaware of what was happening in the skies, Jasper and Worminus started getting ready for their journey.

First, a bag, made from the skin shed from Worminus, was placed around Jasper's body, which held the blip blops.

Secondly, a rope which had quickly been made from strong grasses growing by the side of the gate and last but not least, the casket containing the stone.

"Isn't the casket going to be too big to go in the bag?" Jasper asked.

"Oh, no, my friend, it has a Hellion magnetic pulse, which can adapt itself to any size."

"Will it harm the stone?"

Worminus smiled. "Nothing can harm the stone, and nothing can harm those who carry it, but if the stone falls into wrong hands, it will self-destruct, then it will be lost to the world forever."

As Worminus placed the stone into Jasper's hand, Jasper felt as though the stone had been placed in his keeping and knew he would never let it go, while at that very same moment, a voice was heard giving out the message.

"Protect the stone and it will protect you, because, Jasper Gabalda, you are the second guardian of the stone, which is entrusted into your safekeeping for the safety of all."

Jasper looked at Worminus but saw that Worminus was looking into space.

"Worminus, Worminus!" shouted Jasper.

Worminus turned his head saying, "It's all right, my friend; according to Armild, we are in this together."

"Was it Armild who was speaking to me?"

Worminus nodded, then added, "Are you ready, my little friend, because we must start out on our journey, climb onto me and I'll take the first part of the journey."

Jasper put his arm around Worminus's head, climbed onto his back, and once Worminus knew that Jasper was in a safe position, he slithered under the gate then asked, "Which way do we go?"

"Up the hill to the wood then turn left, follow the road till it reaches the river."

"Okay, let's do it," was the reply as the pair began their journey.

Chapter Thirty-Four
Their Journey Begins

Jasper was amazed how strong and quick Worminus travelled along the ground; at this rate, they could be in London by the second morrow.

With gliding movements, the snake travelled on, only interrupted with, 'Are you all right, Wormy' from Jasper, resting on his strong neck.

As the sun rose higher in the sky, they found themselves at the side of the river, and as Jasper carefully lowered himself to the ground, a wind blew through the branches of a tree making the air feel chilly.

Looking up to see what could have brought on the atmospheric change, Jasper asked, "Can't see any clouds, can you, Wormy?"

Worminus shifted his head. "That's strange, I can't see any clouds either, but it feels as though there is something flying about which is upsetting the atmosphere; let's go further downriver to a place where it will be easier to cross…"

"I'll walk; you have carried me far enough," said Jasper.

"No need to do that, just stay on my back."

"If you say so," said Jasper.

"Yes, I do. I'm the leader of this part of the expedition."

With Worminus in charge, Jasper felt happy, knowing he would need every ounce of strength when they finally reached the Sewer Region; so once again, Jasper climbed onto Worminus and off they went…

The sound of the river was getting louder as the two friends headed down the riverbank, and as they looked for a place to cross, Worminus stopped in his tracks hissing.

"The river has disappeared."

"Don't be silly, Wormy, rivers don't just disappear." Then he shrieked, "It's a waterfall, what are we going to do?"

Because he had never seen a waterfall, Worminus couldn't give an answer.

After thinking for a cess, Jasper decided the best thing to do was to see how far down the waterfall they had to travel, and as they looked over the edge, Jasper saw a large wall of rock going all the way down to where the water disappeared into the ground.

Hurrying back to Worminus, Jasper said, "I don't like it, Wormy; the sides of the waterfall are full of rocks and it's steep."

"Don't worry, Jasper, there isn't a problem," said Worminus, "because we have the magic stone; nothing can go wrong."

As the pair were making plans for getting down the waterfall, in the skies a platoon of meldoes could be seen, where Meldoe 4 using his long view detector saw the waterfall. Turning to the platoon, Meldoe 4 commanded them to fly further over to their left side to investigate, and then he saw WHAT HE HAD COME TO CAPTURE.

Touching his receptor, he gave out the order.

“Platoon at the ready. Smeldewok Gabalda and his companion are directly in our sights. Fly in a circle, make ready for descent; 20, 22, 31 plus 34 fly, into the centre of the formation. On the command of drop, descend, quickly.”

The movement in the sky made Jasper look up and what he saw made him freeze with horror.

Turning to Worminus, Jasper shouted, “Wormy, the Grubber’s spies have spotted us!” Then something magical happened.

A rainbow appeared above the waterfall creating a coloured mist glowing with intense brightness, and every second, it grew bigger till it covered the waterfall and hid the friends from view…

The pair looked at one another in astonishment then, with a ‘quick onto my back, Jasper’, the pair moved to the edge of the waterfall.

Chapter Thirty-Five
Mist and Meldoes

The mist, which had suddenly appeared, stopped the meldoes in their tracks. Meldoe 4 turned to the platoon giving out the order.

"We'll descend as soon as the mist disappears to carry out the operation." And just as though the mist had heard the words, it magically moved upwards causing the platoon to fly higher and higher, till, from out of nowhere, a giant puff of wind blew the mist over the meldoes.

As panic set in, Meldoe 4 gave out another order.

"Move to the right-wing side as quickly as possible and keep moving."

The heaviness in the meldoes' wings from the mist made their flight slower, the ones carrying U.N.O.C. were tiring rapidly as the weight of the covers with the weight of their wings was dragging them downwards, which made four of the meldoes drop out of sight, then, the magical mist seemed to have a mind of its own.

Rising and falling, it hid Jasper and Worminus from the meldoes, making their mission of capturing of the duo impossible.

Meldoe 4 began to feel worried; if he failed to return without the pair, it would be the Time Zone for him, so the order was given.

"Platoon, retrace the flight path back to the nearest ground cover."

The strain was beginning to tell on the meldoes; the cloud seemed to be pushing them back, but all knew was that they had to follow orders, and as the receptor of Meldoe 4 began to crackle, the voice of Meldoe 2 came over the airwaves.

"Progress report needed for the Grubber, state your position, over and out."

Meldoe 4 knowing that there was no getting away from the trouble they were in had to deliver the report.

"Meldoe 2, we are being forced back by a vapour, four of the platoon are lost, and there are no sightings of Smeldewok Gabalda and his companion, over and out." The airwaves went dead, and as the Meldoes looked at their leader, a voice broke the silence.

"Meldoe 2 to Meldoe 4, message from the Grubber."

"Carry on, complete the task, and do not return without Smeldewok Gabalda and the creature, over and out."

Meldoe 4 turned towards the platoon with the order.

"Whatever the cost, we have to fly through the mist; the smeldewok and his companion must be caught. Prepare to descend as quickly as possible through the cloud."

As the platoon turned to its head side, the cold from the mist struck them as they flew through the cloud; the only thing to do was to try and float through the atmosphere, as slowly as they could, which was absolutely impossible; the nearer they got to the land, the quicker they dropped.

Meldoe 4 watched in horror as more of his platoon disappeared leaving him with only twenty meldoes; now the only thing which could possibly save him was to capture the smeldewok with the few personnel he had left…

Ordering the platoon to descend, the remaining meldoes flew downwards into the mist, and as they struggled through the vapour, at the side of the waterfall, the two friends were ready to carry on with their journey.

Chapter Thirty-Six
Back to the Sewer Region

While the two stood at the side of the waterfall, the mist began changing colour into a deep shade of blue, and the pouch which held the stone was surrounded by a blue aura. Jasper gasped, "Look, look, Worminus, look at the pouch, what's happening?"

At that very same moment, through the haze a tall slim being appeared giving the message, "Carry the light," then quickly disappeared.

Speaking in a hushed tone Worminus told Jasper, "Armild is with us and protecting us, so we have to carry on." And because of what had happened, the pair bravely walked towards the edge of the waterfall.

Looking down at the steep rocky incline to the floor of the ravine, Jasper asked, "How are we going to make it to the bottom?"

"Stand still, my friend," was the answer as once again rising to his full height, Worminus split himself in half, wrapped himself around his friend telling him, "lie still, Jasper, off we go."

As they began their journey down the waterfall, Jasper cried, "Please, Wormy, let's get this over with as quickly as possible. I'm standing on my head." But Worminus just carried on slithering downwards as quickly as he could, only stopping when he had reached a boulder, protruding from the bank.

"Why have we stopped?" wailed Jasper.

"Because, I'm your travel carrier, leave it up to me."

"Fair enough," came the answer from Jasper in a voice that sounded as though he had a tummy full of bubbles.

Worminus thinking for a moment then decided that if he hung down from the boulder, his length would take him to the next level. So Worminus said, "Close your eyes, Jasper, and don't start wriggling."

"All right, I won't," was the muffled reply.

Slithering to the edge of the boulder, Worminus made sure that the end of his tail was secure under a rock, then, threw himself forward and when his head was a foot away from the ground, gave a sudden lurch, slithered along in a zigzag movement as Jasper inside Worminus could hear the sound of water, which made him feel sad for his friend.

How could they carry on with their journey if Worminus hated getting wet?

Back came the reply, "Don't worry, little friend, getting wet is not going to hurt." And as Worminus looked for the easiest route to help them on their way, he saw there was a gully running all the way down to the bottom of the ravine, and as he looked again saw it wasn't a gully but an open pipe submerged into the rock. Wow, how amazing; this would make their journey much easier.

Sending the thought to Jasper, 'Hold on, this is going to be the slide of your life', Worminus put his head into the pipe, pushed his body inside and started to slide, slowly at first, then faster and faster, till they reached the bottom of the ravine, and as they slid out of the pipe, Worminus straightened his body and blew Jasper out of his nostrils.

A very shaken up Jasper asked, "Hubbly bubbly, what a ride, can we do that again?"

"Reptilius Senilius, the answer is no; do you want me to have a Snak attack?"

Getting to the bottom of the waterfall and escaping from the meldoes made the pair feel really good, but Jasper sensed that the noise and spray from the waterfall was causing Worminus to worry.

Standing up with a 'Sit there, Worminus, I'll see what I can do', Jasper walked towards the waterfall, and as he looked through the spray, there in front of him was a big black hole, which was the opening to an underground tunnel…

Looking inside the entrance, Jasper could see that there was a wide passageway running into the blackness, and although the sound of the waterfall could still be heard, the inside looked dry; how Jasper wished that he had his UVI with him, so that he could see further into the darkness, as once again a message came from Worminus. "Don't bother about your UVI; give me ten cesses, I will come and take a look." Knowing that Worminus didn't really like water, Jasper started to make his way back to help his friend to get under the waterfall and into the tunnel and once he got back, told Worminus about the tunnel's entrance.

"It will not take more than a few cesses to get to the tunnel, and once we are inside, the meldoes will not be able to see us…"

With a gulp, Worminus answered, "Okay, let's go."

Jasper saw as Worminus moved across the wet ground, that he was struggling with the dampness and wasn't a happy snake, and while he wondered how to help his friend a wonderful idea popped into his mind…

Knowing that time was moving on and no matter how dangerous things might become, they had to get into the tunnel for their safety. Jasper looked at Worminus telling him, "Worminus, the best way to get through all this wet and dampness is for you to wrap yourself around me, and then I can carry you."

"Good idea, Jasper, but how will it work? I'm so big and you're so small."

Jasper grinned. "No Problems, only Solutions."

"Can you make a slip knot in your tail?"

"Why?"

"If you slip the knot around my neck, wrap the rest of yourself around my body, anything leftover I will twist around my arm then I can walk through the entrance without you touching the floor."

"Reptilius Senilius, let's get on with it."

Worminus, wishing he was only the weight of an ordinary worm, started the winding business, while Jasper stood as still as he could, and when Worminus was well and truly all wound up, something unusual happened.

Jasper felt as light as a feather; instead of walking, they were lifted up on a wave of warm air and floated into the tunnel.

Jasper could not understand the magical experience they had just gone through, but as Worminus unravelled himself from around his friend, he once again reminded Jasper that they were being protected by Armild, and as they sat down to rest, both knew they were safely hidden by the mist and the waterfall from the rest of the world, which made Worminus know that without a shadow of doubt, all would be well.

Chapter Thirty-Seven
The Meldoes' Plan

While the pair was resting in the safety of the tunnel, Meldoe 4 was preparing to put a plan into action. It was impossible to cover the journey on foot, which meant that the platoon would have to fly back to the Dartford Tunnel, so gathering the meldoes together, Meldoe 4 gave out the order.

"Make sure all flying equipment is free from the sticky cloud substance as we start our flight back to the Dartford Tunnel immediately."

Knowing this mission was going to put them in danger, Meldoe 50 spoke up for his comrades, "What will the Grubber do to us if we do not succeed?"

Meldoe 4 screeched.

"Not succeed and not succeed, there is no question of not succeeding. If you can't fulfil your role, you must leave the Grubber's army and walk the earth level alone." This made Meldoe 50 know that they must obey the order.

Waiting for the sticky substance on their wings to dry and as the order 'Lift off' rang out, the platoon began their journey into what they knew could be banishment and demotion, and as they struggled in their flight, Meldoe 4 barked out, "To your left-wing side, there is the river where we must arrive in the next 100 cesses. Push yourselves to fly faster and quicker."

Meldoe 50 being the eldest could feel a tingling sensation in his right wing which was causing him to lose smoothness in his flight, and as he saw the motorway below him, he shrieked, "I can't make it; I can't make it!"

"Then don't," came back the chilling reply, and with this, Meldoe 4 manoeuvred his zapping appliance into position, pushed the button, making Meldoe 50 disappear like a fast moving blob onto the motorway below.

After what they had just witnessed and 'Fly on, fly on' was the command, the meldoes dare not do any other; they knew they had to get back into the region.

Flying in formation, they could see, below them, at the side of a forest a river, and as this was the best place for them to rest and gain strength for carrying out their dangerous mission, the command of 'Drop' was given.

Swooping downwards, they landed one after the other till they were all safely on the ground, then Meldoe 4 commanded, "Listen carefully because your safety will depend on this plan. We will stay here till darkness falls, then take off in pairs, 30 cesses between each.

"Our flight path will be over London, flying into the Dartford Tunnel to the third cover. The first pair inside the tunnel will have the task of removing the cover which will be carried out, by fastening the bites to the cover and dragging it open, which must be accomplished or we will not be able to enter into the Sewer Region.

"Lots will be drawn for the ones who are to be responsible for this task…

"Once inside the Sewer Region, two of you will be in charge of closing down the eyes in Corridor Wok, and the rest of the platoon will stop all Black Clocks.

"Get into your sleeping positions to be ready for the morrow."

With fear churning inside them, the meldoes found the nearest tree where they could rest then suspended themselves in an upside-down position to wait for the night and the journey, which would lead them into the hardest most dangerous time of their lives.

Chapter Thirty-Eight
The Tunnel's Secret

As the meldoes slept, Jasper and Worminus rested so that they would be ready to start out on the next part of their journey.

Both were so happy that they were safe inside the tunnel but wondered what mysteries lay in its depths.

"At least, it's dry," said the rather relieved worm.

"At least, we are safe," said Jasper.

To which, Worminus answered, "We'll always be safe, while we have Armild." And with that thought in their minds, they couldn't wait to see where the tunnel would lead them.

The inky blackness made Jasper wish that he had his UVI, which would have made it easier for him to lead Worminus through the tunnel. So with, 'I'll go first, then you can follow', and an 'okay, let's go' from Worminus, the pair started off.

Moving into the darkness, Jasper's eyes got used to the gloom, he could see that the tunnel stretched far into the distance, and knowing that they must get through the tunnel, as quickly as they could, he said, "Come on, Wormy, let's get going."

Worminus stretched his body into a long line and began following Jasper into the darkness; the only sound was that of water coming from the waterfall, which was making Jasper feel uneasy; how could they possibly continue if they couldn't see what lay in front of them?

As if in answer to Jasper's thoughts, from out of nowhere, a tiny light appeared.

"What's that, Wormy?" whispered Jasper, then Worminus gasped.

"Reptilius Senilius, that light belongs to 'the Wormy glows' a part of my family, who I thought were extinct!"

"What's extinct?" Jasper asked.

"Creatures who are not around anymore; they were around when I went to Rome, but they must have gone underground."

Jasper was just about to ask another question when he saw in the distance another light, but this time, it was blue.

"Wormy, look there's a blue one, what sort is that?"

"That will be an Indi glow, if I remember rightly."

Then, as if by magic, one by one, the Wormy glows' lights lit up the tunnel, making Worminus whisper, "It's the work of Armild."

While they both stared at the Wormy glows, Jasper felt a surge of power from the stone which was telling him, "Carry on with your journey; no harm will come to you."

Jasper now knew as they walked further into the tunnel that 'no matter what danger they would encounter, they would always be safe.'

Both friends were feeling exhausted. Jasper felt so sorry for Worminus; at least, he had legs to walk on, but Worminus had no legs at all, and the tunnel seemed to stretch forever in the darkness with no end in sight.

"Let's rest awhile, little friend," said the worm.

Jasper nodded, answering quietly, "Just a little while, Wormy, we have got to get to the end of the tunnel as quickly as we can." As they rested, all they could hear was silence, which made them realise they had travelled downwards into what appeared to be a very deep cave.

Looking around, the lights from the Wormy glows showed them that the walls of the cave glistened with stones of many different shades, which at one time must have been caused by drops of minerals, and even though they were deep inside the tunnel, the earth felt fresh and clean. It was such a magical place that both of them wished they could stay till they felt stronger but knew that they had to carry on.

Moving forward, they could not see a beginning or an end, either in front or behind them, making both of them wonder how much further they had to go.

Because Jasper travelled much quicker than Worminus, he had to stop, and while he waited for Worminus to catch up Jasper heard a sound that was vaguely familiar.

Hearing the sound again, Jasper shouted, "Can you hear it?"

Worminus stopped, put his head to the ground and said, "Yes, there was a throbbing noise." Looking at Jasper, Worminus said, "I can hear it, what do you think could be making such a noise?"

Jasper answered, "If it wasn't so stupid, I would say, it sounds like the air conditioning system in the Sewer Region."

Worminus slithered up to Jasper looking at him with hope in his bright green eyes, as they both thought:

Could it possible that we are heading in the right direction to our JOURNEY'S END?

Chapter Thirty-Nine
The Meeting in the Tunnel

The tunnel looked quite welcoming as all the Wormy and Indie glows shone like stars in the gloom; with the excitement of finding out what else they might see, the little travellers moved on, forgetting how tired they were.

While they carried on exploring from nowhere came a blast of cool air, and in front of them, a hole appeared in the ground.

“What next?” whispered Jasper, his words echoing around and around the hole.

“What are we going to do about this?” asked Worminus.

Then Jasper came up with the idea.

“Let’s drop something into it; if it makes a sound, we might be able to tell how deep it is.”

“What with?” asked Worminus.

“Look around for something,” said Jasper.

While Worminus was looking around, a Wormy glow appeared at the side of Jasper’s foot, and in its light, Jasper saw a round-shaped object covered with glowing stripes of red and green; in fact, Jasper thought it resembled a rather large blip blop.

Worminus looking at it, said, “Pick it up.”

"I can't," wailed Jasper.

"You will have to, because I haven't got any fingers."

Jasper shut his eyes, stretched out his hand and immediately the object rolled into his hand, giving him such a shock that he nearly dropped it.

As they looked at it, they saw the thing had a slit on the top of its head with something poking through.

"Pull it out, Jasper; you have got fingers."

"I'll poke it out with my nail."

Then the unbelievable happened.

"Be careful whoever you are because I'm delicate!" shrieked the ball-like thing.

Jasper was so surprised to hear it speak that he nearly dropped the thing on to the floor; as once again, the thing spoke.

"Just pull it out."

Jasper looked at Worminus who mouthed, "You'd better pull it out."

Jasper with the tip of his nail caught hold of what was sticking out of the slit, gave a gentle pull and out popped a worm-type object, covered in numbers; whatever it was, it was certainly scary.

The worm-type object had two little eyes, which kept on blinking so that you didn't know if they were opened or closed, also, two ears which flapped backwards and forwards making sound waves, and as the tiny creature looked up to see what it thought was a very strange pair, the sound waves from its ears made a high-pitched sound, which turned into the words:

"I'm Thingy thing; who are you two, tell me your names please. I've told you who I am so just be quick about it, and whatever your name is, DON'T DROP ME!"

"I'm Jasper and I won't," said Jasper.

"I'm Worminus, and no, he won't," said Worminus.

As the thing now knew who the two were, it stopped its rolling movement, and while it lay in his hand Jasper moved over to look down the shaft wondering how they could possibly continue their journey down a hole.

Worminus hissed, "Don't worry, little friend, something will tell us what to do." Then the thing screeched again.

"Hey, Jasper, whoever you are, stop squeezing me, uncurl your hand and stop digging that long nail into my back."

"Sorry, Thingy, didn't realise what I was doing. I was just thinking about something."

"Can you explain what you were thinking about?" insisted the bossy little object.

"We are travelling to the place called the Sewer Region and we really can't get any further till we know how deep is the hole."

"There is only one answer to that, stop being stupid and drop me down the hole."

Jasper, who had never come across such a bossy object before and certainly didn't like the word stupid, was just about to say something when Worminus, who knew what Jasper was thinking, moved in front of the little smeldewok sending the thoughts, "Keep your mouth shut, or Thingy won't help us."

Realising that Worminus was right, Jasper asked, "If I drop you down the hole, you might get harmed and what good will that do?"

Thingy, thinking that Jasper was being silly about him being harmed, said, "Just place me on top of the hole, press the spot on my head, I'll unwind all the way to the bottom, then come back to the top and tell you how deep it is."

"How can you?"

"Because I've got numbers on my body and not only that, my body can stretch for miles."

"Hey, that's good, isn't it, Wormy?"

Worminus nodded, then, asked, "What's your proper title?"

The round ball puffed up with pride, announcing, "I'm an Inch worm."

"Of course, you are," said a smiling Worminus. "I should have known that you are another branch of the family who is not extinct."

The Inch worm looked deeply at Worminus asking, "What branch of the family do you belong to?"

"Mother was of the earth side and Father was of the grass."

Thingy nodded his head saying, "Well, that explains why you are so large."

Jasper feeling anxious, shouted at the pair, "Okay, okay, you two, stop talking, more action."

"Right," both said together.

Then more and more things happened.

Chapter Forty
The Hole in the Ground

Going to the edge, Jasper looked at Thingy, as Thingy looked back saying, "Silly one, stand me on the edge and drop me down the hole, and when I say now, do it. Get it?"

Worminus knew the quickest way to make Thingy go down the shaft was to blow on Thingy, and when Thingy said 'NOW', Worminus gave the biggest blow he could.

The thing propelled itself out of Jasper's hand to the edge of the hole, then with a fizzy noise, it disappeared over the edge, but just as quickly as it disappeared, it reappeared announcing to the waiting pair, "I'm just short."

"How much short?"

"Well, I'd know if I had a length of something."

All of a sudden, the pouch began to glow.

Jasper gasped, and as the pouch began glowing even more brightly, Jasper knew he had to open it.

There inside was the thing they needed, A ROPE, and at that very same moment, Worminus knew no matter ever whatever else could happened to them, Armild would still look after them.

Pulling the rope out of the pouch, Jasper laid it on the ground as Thingy looked at it, shrieking in his shrill voice,

"That's just the right length I need, from me to the bottom of the shaft."

"Oh, then it's not too deep," Jasper stated.

"Course, it's deep, that's the length of the rope I need and then I have to extend myself, you silly thing."

Jasper's usually twinkly face took on a scowl. "I know it's a good idea, but how are we going to do it?"

Thingy screeched, "Silly one, tie your rope around my head, drop me down the shaft, and when I've reached the bottom, you can slide down then once you've done that, it will be Worminus's turn."

"Will you be able to take two of us at the same time?"

"Of course, I can, I'm very strong."

"All right, Thingy, let's go."

Jasper tied the rope around Thingy, then, with a nod of his large head, Worminus, gave out the order, "Jasper, stand still, you Thingy, into your place." And as Thingy moved to the edge of the shaft, Worminus split himself in half, wrapped himself around Jasper, blew through his nostrils and Thingy flew down the hole.

Once Thingy reached the bottom, he waited and watched as Worminus, with Jasper inside him, started sliding down the rope, and once they reached Thingy, Worminus unwound himself from Jasper as Thingy screeched, "Let go of the rope!"

Immediately, Jasper did what Thingy told him and let go of the rope as Thingy flew back up the shaft and once he was at the top, flapped his ears with the message.

"On your way, you two."

Jasper opened his mouth to thank the strange little creature, but Thingy stopped him by screeching, "No need for thanks, just go through the door at the end of the tunnel and bring back hope to Sewer Region!" Then he disappeared from view.

The pair couldn't believe their eyes; Thingy had disappeared as suddenly as he had appeared.

What was going to happen next?

After their long slide down the rope and the departure of Thingy, they stopped for a cess to get their bearings before starting off on the next part of their journey.

Moving forward, they could see in the distance another tunnel, and as Worminus lifted his head, he saw something shining.

The more he looked, he could see that it definitely was the glow of a light.

Turning to his friend, he excitedly told him, "Jasper, I can see a light, that must be where the tunnel ends, so come on let's go." As Worminus finished speaking, to their amazement, the ground started moving carrying them forward, and before they knew what was happening, they found themselves in the middle of the light looking at a door.

The door was big and black, but there was nothing that would open it. Jasper looking worried turned to Worminus saying, "What are we going to do; we've got so far and aren't going to get any further."

Then, as if in answer to the question, the voice of Armild could be heard, telling Worminus, "Blow through your nostrils." And as Worminus blew and blew, a mighty gush of air hit the door, which began opening.

The pair stood transfixed; how they wanted to go through the door, but if they did, it would lead them into the unknown and this would be scary.

Worminus gently nudged his loving comrade saying, "Come on, Jasper, we have to do this." Then once again, the voice of Armild broke the stillness.

"Go with courage; I will be with you every step of the way."

Looking at each other, they knew that Armild would always be with them; so bravely, they stepped through the door, which slowly closed behind them.

Looking around, they saw they were in another tunnel exactly like the one they had left. Jasper stopped; he felt as if he was waking up from a bad dream as memories kept flooding into his mind only to disappear a cess later.

Always concerned for his friend, Worminus waited for Jasper to make the next move, and as Jasper turned back to look at the door, he couldn't believe where they were…

"This is it, Wormy, this is the boundary to my homeland."

So, Worminus asked, "Where do we go from here, my friend?"

"I don't know," answered Jasper. "We were never allowed to come this far."

"How many cesses ago was that?"

"I can't really remember, but it seems as though it's been going on for the whole of my life.

Lifting up his enormous head, his bright eyes looking into Jasper's, Worminus smiled as only a snake can smile while giving out the message, "All will be well, my friend; we must continue because I have to get you home."

Chapter Forty-One
Another Corridor, Another Door

Travelling through the cave-like passage, the air had a peculiar feeling to it as though nothing living had travelled along its way for a very long time, and as they moved forward, they could hear a faint thudding sound.

Wondering what or where the sound was coming from, Worminus stretched out his long neck as far as he could, and when he couldn't stretch any further, out came the words, "Keep going, Jasper, there's another corridor in front of us."

Hearing this, the little smeldewok began to cover the ground as though he was running in a race, and keeping up with Jasper's long thin legs became impossible for Worminus; the faster Jasper moved, the more he disappeared out of sight.

Thinking that he might have lost Jasper, Worminus didn't know what to do; he couldn't bear to think he might never see his friend again, then, something weird happened.

Little wheels sprouted out of his body, and before he knew it, the wheels started spinning and off he went; so that in next to no time, he had caught up with Jasper, who by this time was sat on the floor with tears running down his face.

Worminus was just about to say something when Jasper looked up to see his best friend.

Jumping up, Jasper threw his arms around his friend saying, "I will never run off again."

Worminus winked saying, "No Problems, only solutions."

Moving down the corridor, Jasper could now see that they were on the boundaries of the Sewer Region, and even though he was feeling excited, he knew he had to remind Worminus to keep out of sight of the all-seeing eyes in the wall, or else they would be in danger.

Walking as quickly and as quietly as they could, they moved along the corridor till they found themselves in front of a wall of solid stone.

In the centre of the stonewall was an archway over a door, and at the top of the archway was a notice which read,

"What do you think it means?"

"I can't think what it means."

After a pause and still looking at the words, Jasper asked, "Do you think there is an EZ one?"

"Well, if there's an EZ one, there must be an EZ two. I wonder if it's some sort of passageway."

The friends, feeling very puzzled, debated all sorts of ideas, passageways, underground walkways; the notice just didn't make sense; the more they tried, the more exasperated they got, and time was against them.

Sitting down, Jasper leaned against the long body of the worm; he was so tired and so cross that they had come so far and it looked as though, this was as far as they were going; then as Worminus looked once again at the notice, the strangest thing happened. Magically, the E moved up to join the T.I.M.

"Look, Jasper," Worminus hissed, "just look at it." And as Jasper focused on the letters, the Z moved downwards to join the O.N.E. Jasper gasped.

"So, this is where it is."

"Where, what is?"

"It's the Time Zone!" shrieked Jasper.

"TIME ZONE, what's that?"

"It's the place where the Grubber has imprisoned many families."

Looking at the door, which once again was a 'Door with nothing to open it', made them worry, but once again, from out of nowhere, a blue mist appeared as the voice of Armild spoke to them.

"Worminus, do as I told you, blow through your nostrils."

Worminus filled up his head with as much breath as he could, turned to the door and blew through his nose so hard that Armild and the blue mist disappeared and the door opened into a tunnel hewn out of solid rock.

Chapter Forty-Two
The Time Zone and Its Secrets

As Jasper and Worminus looked down the tunnel, they could see that steps had been cut out of the rock face, which led down into what looked like intense blackness.

Jasper froze; he dare not move.

"I'm scared, Worminus; I'm scared."

"Don't be, Jasper, because we are being protected."

And as Jasper started to panic again, a blue mist shone into the gloom, lighting up their surroundings.

"Armild has done it again," said Worminus. "Just put your faith in the wise one."

"I will, Worminus, I will."

Starting their descent, Jasper went down step by step, while Worminus slithered over the top of every step, which made it easier for his long body to travel downwards into the intense blackness.

The further down into the darkness they went; besides it being impossible to see anything in front of them, it was also eerily silent making Jasper whisper the question, "How much further have we to go?"

"We must carry on no matter how difficult it becomes," was the answer. "Just remember that Armild is protecting us," replied Worminus making Jasper know that everything would be all right.

Down and down into the bowels of the earth they went; as the aura of the blue light cast eerie shadows on the wall turning their silhouettes into two huge monsters, Worminus said, "Let's carry on to where ever it leads, leads, leads." His last word echoed into the darkness.

The stillness in the stairway felt oppressive, and the only sounds that could be heard came from Jasper's feet and the slithering of the worm as they manoeuvred their way down the rock hewn steps.

Nowhere, either above or below ground, had the pair ever been in a place like the one they were in at this moment, but to turn back until they had achieved what they had set out to do was unthinkable.

Moving down the rock steps as quick as they could, they found themselves in a large chamber, the biggest they had ever entered, which had been carved out of rock.

It stretched as far as the eye could see, and the atmosphere was so cold it was as if they were stood in the middle of a glacier while the only comforting thing was the blue light.

As their eyes got used to the gloom, they could see bundles of rags laid all over the floor of the cavern.

"What do you think they are?" Worminus whispered.

As if in answer to the question, one of the bundles moved.

"Look it moved," said Jasper. "Whatever it is, must need help, stay where you are, Worminus, it will be much easier for me to move about, because I've got legs."

Worminus nodded knowing it made sense, but if anything endangered the little smeldewok, he would move through the bundles to rescue his friend.

Walking carefully over to the bundle, Jasper stretched out his hand and moved a corner of the rags, and the face that stared up at him was the sad tired face of Granpo Onkle.

Jasper moved the rags further back. "Granpo Onkle, Granpo Onkle, is it you?"

A weak faltering voice said, "Jasper."

With tears rolling down his face, the little smeldewok gently gave the answer that Granpo Onkle had so longed to hear.

"Yes, it is."

Jasper put both his arms around Granpo Onkle who whispered quietly, "Thank goodness, you have found us; time is running out." Jasper could now see what a terrible situation this was.

"Are all these bundles smeldewoks?"

Granpo Onkle nodded.

"Where are my parents?"

Granpo Onkle with a mighty effort, lifted his head, calling out, "Tenora, Tenora, where are you?"

Situated in the furthest corner of the cavern, a voice no more than a whisper, cried, "I'm here, Onkle, over here."

Worminus hissed, "What are you waiting for, go to your father."

Moving through the rows of bewildered smeldewoks, Jasper came to the bundle which contained the most loved being that had always been there for him, and as he pulled back the rags, Jasper saw for the first time, his father.

Lifting him in his arms, his father spoke. "My son, your mother is right by my side." Jasper could not believe that he would once again see the mother who he adored then, bending down, he moved the rest of the rags, to see the beautiful face of his mother looking back at him.

Here were his parents, who had always been there for him; now he was here for them.

Watching the scene from the entrance of the chamber, Worminus knew if ever the stone and his gift were needed, it was now.

Chapter Forty-Three
The Rescue

A voice quickly joined by the rest asked, "Please have you any food?"

Jasper was glad that he had some of his blip blops, but looking around, he became worried that there wouldn't be enough blip blops to go around.

Once more, the blue aura appeared as the pouch, on his side, got heavier and heavier, and looking down, Jasper saw that the pouch was overflowing with blip blops.

Armild had done it again. Enough food for everyone.

Jasper, turning towards his family and friends who had now enough strength to sit up, looked towards Worminus saying, "This, my friends, is Worminus Snak, the greatest creature I have ever known, who has become my friend, and my mentor saved my life and promised to help me overthrow our enemies, to restore our king to his righteous place, as the head of our domain."

And while this was being said, a hundred pair of eyes smiled through the gloom at Worminus, while Worminus looked back at them through tear-filled eyes. A quavering voice, from the top right-hand corner of the cavern, said, "The king is here. I fear he is very weak and may not live till the morrow."

Worminus turned to Jasper telling him, "Follow me and bring the stone."

Moving through the mass of bodies on the cavern floor, they reached the place where their beloved king lay.

Kneeling down by his side, Worminus said to Jasper, "Open the pouch." Jasper opened it slowly but was unsure what to do next, till Worminus told him.

"Bring out the casket, open the lid and bring out the stone." And as the stone was brought out of the pouch, it brought with it a dazzling light which lit up the darkness of the Time Zone.

Looking at the light became too painful for the smeldewoks who had lived in darkness for such a long time, until, the words 'Hold up the stone so the light can fall on your king' were heard, then, one by one, as they lifted their faces, all waited in silence to see what sort of a miracle was going to happen.

Holding the star-shaped stone, Jasper could feel the stone's vibration sending lights twirling, not only on the king but on every smeldewok.

And while the twinkling lights filled them with a wondrous strength, the face of King Cuthbert, the kind, appeared.

Slowly and hesitantly, he started moving, getting stronger with each light that touched his body, till once again, the king stood in front of his subjects, and the day the little smeldewoks had longed for had finally happened.

Once again, there was hope, for these troubled little creatures…

With the stone held tightly in his hand, Jasper turned to Worminus with, 'Thank you for your wondrous gift', as the answer was given.

"Not only have I been given the gift but remember, Jasper, that you are also the second guardian of the stone."

Jasper, feeling overwhelmed, that he had been entrusted with something so special, gently placed the remarkable stone back in its pouch, put his arms around his friend and cried.

Lifting his head, he saw his parents, standing at the side of him, and while he hugged them every smeldewok, who were now renewed with energy, knew that the end was in sight for the Grubber, and the atmosphere in the cavern was filled with hope.

Those who thought they would never be reunited with the ones they had left behind were now ready to play their part in whatever would be decided.

King Cuthbert with Jasper and his father moved over to the large worm ready to work out a plan which would help them in their fight against the Grubber.

A decision had to be made and made quickly, and when all had been decided and the plan was set in place, King Cuthbert announced:

"Jasper and Worminus will lead us to freedom."

With the shouts of 'Aye!' from the all the smeldewoks, King Cuthbert outlined the plan.

"Four of us will lead the way into the corridors, and with all the risks that have to be taken, the weak and elderly will wait here till it is safe to leave, once the sqones are released, then the rest of you will carry out the next part of the plan."

As the smeldewoks watched the four move over to the steep rock steps leading out of the cavern, tears filled the eyes of each gentle creature, all wanting the plan to succeed.

Now all they had to do was wait.

Chapter Forty-Four
The Uprising Begins

The four started to climb upwards out of the cavern; every step they climbed seemed to become steeper and dangerous, especially for Worminus who could only slither along on his body…

Helping each other, they moved over each step with care, till at last, they were standing in one of the corridors.

Worminus, remembering all that Jasper had said about the eyes in the walls, stretched himself upwards till he could touch the eyes, then, with a flick of his head, moved them to face in the opposite direction…

Moving quietly down the corridor, Jasper noticed another corridor turning to the right and not daring to speak, in case of the sound of his voice carried, pointed in its direction, and as they stopped and wondered if it would be safe to continue, it was then that Worminus had a bright idea.

If he could move his head, around the bend into the corridor, he would be able to see if the coast was clear and that there was nothing that would harm them.

Stretching his neck as far as it would go, one half of Worminus stayed with the group, and the other half of his body turned down the corridor.

The group were amazed as they watched Worminus all wondering if he would ever be a straight Worminus again, but with his magical gift of knowing what others were thinking, pulled his neck back, giving the message, "Don't worry, the coast is clear." And hearing these words, all began moving very quietly into the corridor.

The corridor was brightly lit, which made them aware they might be seen by the Grubber's spies so, once again, Worminus reached up and turned the eyes in the walls in the opposite direction.

Keeping themselves in a tight knit group, they moved quickly towards the end of the corridor but stopped as they saw a notice which read:

'AIR WAVES STUDIO.'

'PLEASE DO NOT ENTER WHILE THE RED LIGHT IS SHOWING.'

The notice was hung over a door in the wall where high up above the sign, a circular window could be seen…

"What are we going to do?" they all asked, looking at Jasper for the answer.

"The only answer is…" replied Jasper.

"Yes?" they all whispered.

"To look through the window."

"But how can we?"

"By me," said Worminus, stretching himself upwards, only to find he was a little too short to see through the window.

Thinking for a moment, Worminus hissed down to Jasper.

"Two heads are better than one, climb up onto my head, then you can look through the window."

"Are you slippery? Cos if you are, I won't be able to get up to the window."

"Just try."

Hearing this, the others got hold of Jasper, gave him a mighty push, pushing him so hard that he whizzed all the way up. Worminus, then, swaying slightly and holding his friends head, remarked, "Well, that's solved one problem, so let's solve the other and look through the window." Jasper wiggled about on Worminus's head to make himself comfortable, which Worminus found annoying, then looked down into a room lined with maps containing charts of the Sewer Region and where a batlike figure of a meldoe sat at a table, speaking through a tube.

Hushing the others to be quiet, Jasper put his ear to the window and as he listened, heard the meldoe give out this message: "All meldoes must return to base…"

"What's happening?" the group asked.

Jasper whispered, "The meldoes have to return back to base, which is not going to make it easy for us to carry out the plan to capture the Grubber."

"What are we going to do?" they all said, and before they had time to ask any more questions, the pouch around Jasper's middle began vibrating, sending out a beam of light and while this was happening, Worminus told Jasper:

"Shine the beam through the window, this will distract the meldoe, then we can then move in, overpower him and take charge…" Jasper nodded.

Moving the pouch up to the window, Jasper shone the light into the meldoes eyes, and as he whispered 'Now',

Worminus dropped down the wall, pushed the door open, propelled Jasper at the meldoe's head, which knocked the meldoe to the floor, and while this was happening the king and Jasper's father dashed into the room, stood the terrified meldoe up on his trembling feet, and the king spoke.

"You will repeat this information into the tube.

"All meldoes must open all gates to the Grubber's quarters. Return back to their pods, immediately. Eyes and clocks to be turned off and shut down and all U.N.O.C. to be collected and placed together outside the Grubber's pod ready for immediate use. This order has to be carried out without delay."

The trembling meldoe gave out the message, as all meldoe in the confines of the Sewer Region wondered what scheme the Grubber had in mind, which not one of them dare question or disobey.

In the Airwaves Studio, the meldoe wondered, *What will become of me if my master finds out what has happened?*

Shall I stay with the captors or stay with the master?

Watching the meldoe's movements and reading its mind Worminus delivered the answer.

"Stay where you are, traitors will not be tolerated." This made the meldoe tremble with fear.

Now all that remained was for Jasper to begin the plan for liberation.

Chapter Forty-Five
The Plan Is Carried Out

Leaving the others to guard the meldoe, Jasper made his way through the silent corridors of the region, and when he arrived at the top of the stairs leading down into the Time Zone, he felt very nervous; how he wished Worminus was with him, but at the same time, he felt something was keeping him safe.

Could it be Armild? If it was, he knew nothing would harm him.

Moving carefully over the steps, down and down he went till once more he found himself in the large cavern of the Time Zone.

In the gloom, hundreds of eyes looked at him, and as he walked towards them, some of the smeldewok reached out from their pile of rags, wanting to know what was happening.

Jasper began, "At the moment, all is well, but we need help to get to the Grubber's pod as quickly and safely as we can; so, I will need four of the strongest, who can work and take orders. You must all decide amongst yourselves who it is to be."

From the back of the crowd, three smeldewoks stepped forward.

"Take us, Jasper; we will do whatever is needed; we are not frightened to die in the attempt to restore our race to the peaceful existence we once knew."

Jasper whispered, "Come with me."

The comforting light from the stone lit up the darkness giving hope to all the poor creatures who had been made to live in this terrible place for such a long time. Jasper turned to the rest of his family and friends and told them, "Soon you will be able to walk the corridors of the Sewer Region without fear."

Leading the four smeldewoks up the steps out of the cavern, Jasper motioned to them to move silently, and once they arrived at the Airwaves Studio, Jasper tapped out the secret signal on its door to let the others know that he had brought some help.

Entering the Airwaves Studio, the atmosphere seemed as though it was trying to tell them to move to the next part of the operation, and as he looked at the meldoe, Worminus told him, "Give the order over the airwaves that a curfew will be imposed till the morrow, and that any meldoe breaking this curfew will be sent to the Time Zone."

Once more, Jasper led the trembling meldoe to the table, giving him a stare which said, 'Don't disobey', and as the speaking tube was placed before him, the meldoe gave out the message.

Jasper quietly asked Worminus, "What are we going to do with our prisoner?"

The answer was, "We are taking him with us; we will use him as our seer in."

Jasper smiled, knowing that his friend always had the right answer, while powerless to do anything to let his comrades really know what was happening, the meldoe decided it would be safer for him to agree to every task his captors gave him, till the time would be right for him to get his revenge.

Once, the message had been given out, it was decided that Worminus would lead the way, and as everyone was leaving the Airwaves Studio, they were determined that before the day was out all smeldewoks would have their birth right restored.

Halfway down the central corridor, the group came across a party of sqones hard at work sweeping the floor, then the king stepped forward and, with a gentle gesture, touched the head of the nearest sqone who stopped work, expecting to see one of his captors give him an order, and when nothing was said, he lifted up his tired little head to find himself looking into the face of King Cuthbert, the kind.

Rattling the heavy chain attached to the rest of the working party, the gang stopped what they were doing and one by one looked up to see, standing in front of them, their king, Jasper and his father who with a smeldewok was holding onto a meldoe and also a rather big wormlike creature.

The little sqones looked at Worminus, and Jasper could see how frightened they were. Moving forward and holding on to Worminus, Jasper told them, how his friend had saved him and was ready to help them all to get rid of the evil Grubber.

At the very same time, that Jasper was telling them about Worminus, the pouch started vibrating, shining beams of light onto the chain that held the sqones together, then, one by one, each link was broken and the little sqones threw their arms around Jasper, making him more determined than ever, to rid his homeland of the terrible monster, the Grubber.

Chapter Forty-Six
Corridor Wok and Beyond

Jasper turned to everyone, telling them to start moving and Worminus who had the amazing gift of putting his head around corners and leaving his body where it was led the party safely, silently and speedily through the dimly lit corridors.

As the group moved along the passageways, at the beginning of one of the corridors, Jasper saw the sign. 'CORRIDOR WOK', here at last was the place where he knew he would find his friends, but as there was hardly any light in the corridor, and as he looked into the gloom, he saw what he thought was an opening in the wall.

Whispering to the others to keep quiet, he walked over to the opening, and as he stepped inside saw that there were lots of cavities in the walls, and the more he looked, he could see that were filled with sleeping smeldewok while other smeldewok sat in silence, around a table…

Not wanting to frighten them, Jasper moved silently into the darkest recess then quietly said, "My friends, my friends, I'm here…"

For a moment, all was still, then as the ones sat at the table turned to see where the voice was coming from, Jasper stepped forward.

With a rush, they surrounded Jasper, touching and holding him as if to convince themselves he was real, and as Jasper raised his hand saying, 'Wake the others', the sleeping smeldewok woke to see the friend that they all loved, standing in front of them.

The atmosphere inside the pod changed from despair to happiness especially as they heard, "My friends, I have brought your king." And as they saw their king step forward, the little creatures were once again filled with hope.

Next it was Worminus's turn, and as Jasper brought Worminus forward, the smeldewok who had never seen anything as big as the worm felt uneasy, till Jasper started telling them about his friend.

"Not only is it me who has got us this far, this is my life saviour, Worminus Snak, who has worked out a clever plan for getting rid of the Grubber."

Hearing this, they all realised that everything was all right because this huge creature who had kept their beloved Jasper safe was ready to fight for their rights.

Worminus, then began to outline his plan.

"We have to divide into three groups.

"The first group will be responsible for stopping all meldoe returning from their mission, from gaining entrance into the region.

"The second group will take the U.N.O.Cs to the end of the corridor leading to the third opening of the Dartford Tunnel, place the covers into a half circle to trap the meldoe. The third group will be the ones to capture the Grubber, but when moving down the corridors, everyone must keep out of sight of the all-seeing eyes."

When it was decided who was to be in each group, the first and second groups started out for the opening of the Sewer Region, while Worminus, Jasper and the rest with their captive set off down the labyrinth of passageways towards the Grubber's pod.

Jasper's group moved quickly down the corridors to the Grubber's pod and the on-duty sqone, TZ 59, working inside the pod heard footsteps; he opened the screen to see King Cuthbert, the kind.

Stepping forward, the king motioned the sqone to keep silent, whispering into his ear, "We are going to take the Grubber captive, so you must act as though nothing strange is happening."

Looking bewildered, the sqone whispered, "But how can this happen?"

"Trust," the king answered, then pushing their captive to the front of the group, the king with a fierce look at the meldoe gave him the order, "Go inside and tell the Grubber that which he has been waiting for is close at hand." While this was happening, TZ 59 looking at what he thought was a monster standing at the side of Jasper, started backing away, until, Jasper whispered, "The worm is an ally and will do everything in its power for the good of the region."

While, inside the pod, a rasping voice pod demanded, "Sqone, what is happening?"

Worminus whispered to the sqone, "Go and tell the Grubber that a messenger has arrived with remarkable news." And as the sqone started walking to enter the Grubber's pod, Jasper and his friends waited for what they had most hoped for, capturing the evil Grubber.

Chapter Forty-Seven
Capturing the Grubber

From inside the pod, the rasping voice of the Grubber could be heard asking, "Yes, what, what, what is going on?"

TZ 59 replied, "There is a messenger, with important news. Show him in."

TZ 59 moved back to the opening, while Jasper and Worminus waiting to strike pushed the captive meldoe into the Grubber's pod…

The pod was warm, stuffy and dimly lit, which made it hard for the anties to clean the fat sluglike body of the Grubber while he lay on his couch, and as the meldoe moved towards the Grubber, Jasper and Worminus watched their prisoner, to see that the meldoe made no false moves…

"Well," went the voice, "come over here where I can see you."

The meldoe bowed, "I am here, master."

"What is the important news?"

"I have brought captives."

On these words, Worminus and Jasper rushed into the pod followed by the rest of their party, and as they quickly surrounded the Grubber, Jasper looked into the Grubber's piggy eyes, telling him, "We are here not to do your bidding, because you are now going to do ours; it is time for you to put right all the wrong you have done."

Jasper, then with an almighty dig, poked the Grubber's mass of fat with his magical nail while, at the same time, the pouch started to vibrate and the light from the stone shone onto the Grubber, who started growing smaller and smaller till all that was left was a rubber ball with piggy eyes who started rolling about, shaking with rage and shouting in a thin squeaky voice, "You will pay for this when my spies arrive!"

Jasper looked down at the now little Grubber, telling him, "Right, you ounce of blubber, be thankful, we haven't rendered you into bucketfuls of goo." Then, turning to the sqones with 'Guard the two prisoners', Worminus, Jasper and the others left the pod to get to the Dartford Tunnel before the meldoes arrived…As the meldoes flew through the skies, out of the sixty meldoes, only ten had returned, and Meldoe 4 couldn't wait to get back to the region.

Although he had failed in the task to capture both, Jasper Gabalda, the worm and the stone, he knew he would never be a failure, because when the time was right, he would take over and rule the Sewer Region.

Giving out the order to 'Keep in twos and fly inside the tunnel to the third drain cover', the platoon swerved to the left and started their descent into the tunnel and the open drain cover.

Even though they were nearly home, they all wondered what punishment the Grubber would give them for not succeeding with the mission.

While three of the sqones waiting inside the drain cover for the return of the meldoes had to pretend that everything was normal – they dare not think of what would happen if the plan went wrong, and as the beat of the meldoes' wings could be heard, Meldoe 4 landed, followed in quick sequence by the rest of the platoon.

Chapter Forty-Eight
The Plan Is Carried Out

Further down the corridor, Worminus had laid the mesh-type cover on the floor, and after this was done, he attached the ends to the all-seeing eyes in the walls creating a hammock-style apparatus, and while all the plans were being carried out, through the hollow echoing corridor the sound of the meldoes' feet could be heard.

Worminus sent a thought out to Jasper.

"As soon as the spies stand on the nets, I'll hit them with my tail, drop on top of them, and then you can tie up the top of the mesh, is that clear?"

"Clear," came back the answer.

As the sound of marching to the call of four steps, three steps, two steps became louder, the meldoes appeared; the order rang out, "Now."

Worminus flicked his tail, gave one great swipe, knocked down the spies, puffed air into his nostrils, blew the net around the meldoes, as Jasper and the rest tied the ends together then, bending down to the spies, Jasper told them, "Now you know what it's like to be on the receiving end of evil doings?"

Meldoe 4 looked at Jasper, thinking, "All is not yet lost." Then he sharply turned his face into the net, snapped an order out to the imprisoned meldoes, and in one cess, the evil bats were all facing the same way, their mouths opened with a flash, as they fastened their metal bites onto the net and with a ripping sound began tearing holes in their prison.

"What now?" cried the smeldewoks, and before Jasper could say anything, the pouch began to vibrate, shining the beam on the net.

With a clanking sound, the sharpened bites of the meldoes fell from their mouths; their plan had come to nothing.

Jasper and his friends picked up each corner of the net, carrying the squirming meldoes, into the Grubber's pod, and as the net was cut open, one by one they were made to stand and face the Grubber where they saw their master, the great Madgoo the Grubber, had turned into a small rubber ball with a pair of very angry eyes.

Jasper turned to the now very scared meldoes saying, "You can see that which has happened to your ruler has happened because, nothing good comes from evil.

"With my friend and life saviour, Worminus Snak, we will banish everything that is evil from the region, so that once again peace and harmony will reign in this domain." The meldoes huddled together wondering what their fate was going to be, and as Worminus moved towards them, the meldoes backed away from the big worm, who stood over the prisoners, shaped his nostrils into one big hole as though he was going to suck them up into his head; a mighty scream escaped from the meldoes.

Smiling, Worminus moved away as the king stepped forward giving out the order, "Bring our comrades out of the confines of the Time Zone, also the rest of the smeldewoks and sqones from their spaces and assemble them down each side of the central corridor." And as the order was carried out, the Grubber and his spies waited to see what their fate would be.

In the huge dark chamber of the Time Zone, the forgotten ones sat together, brother to brother, grandparents, children, mothers and fathers; all were waiting for news which would tell them that they would climb the steps to freedom.

As footsteps were heard at the top of the steep flight of steps, all went silent.

If the plan hadn't worked, who were the ones who would be entering the chamber?

The atmosphere was tense; whimpering could be heard from some of the little woklings, and all eyes turned towards the steps.

Into view came two of the smeldewoks, who had chosen to go with Jasper.

The cry went up, "Give us the news!"

The smeldewoks with joy in their voice delivered the news:

"WE ARE FREE!"

Chapter Forty-Nine
The Story Ends

As the first smeldewok came into the Time zone, he gave out Jasper's message.

"All must leave the Time Zone to stand in the corridors."

The smeldewoks, who had been made captives, could not believe that the time had finally come, when at last they would be able to live together freely and safely.

With the young ones helping mothers and fathers, grandmas and granddads, they started the climb up the long steep steps to freedom, while in another part of the region, two of Jasper's party hurried towards the quarters of the off-duty sqones to tell them of the wonderful news.

Tapping quietly on the sliding screen of the Ezze, the smeldewoks waited till they could hear movements, as a sad face looked through the opening asked, "Is there trouble?" The reply came back.

"No, may we enter?"

Entering the Ezze, they were surrounded by the little sqones.

"What is it?" whispered TZ 89.

"There has been an uprising, and Jasper Gabalda has overthrown the Grubber."

Staring at the smeldewoks, the little creatures shouted, "How has this happened?"

"Follow us into the central corridor where you will find out."

Walking into the main corridor, the sound of cheering could be heard, as smeldewoks of all ages appeared, until each side of the corridor was filled with happy creatures.

Then footsteps were heard.

Coming down the central corridor flanked by sqones, meldoes were being led to the Grubber's pod looking like little frightened little mice, and as they were marched up to the pod and entered, they were ordered.

"Assemble yourselves together with your leader for your retreat from the Sewer Region."

On the order of 'Lift', they picked up the couch, on which lay the once mighty Grubber as the king delivered the final ultimatum.

"By my decree, you are banished from the Sewer Region; take all that is evil with you never to return again."

The once mighty meldoes, carrying the little rubber ball who had once been the Grubber, moved down the corridor, to the door through which Jasper and Worminus had entered into the Sewer Region but now had become the exit to a deep dark mysterious region. They heard a voice saying, "Depart with your evil to troll the depths and walk in darkness for all eternity." While a rushing wind, swept through the corridor, blowing the Grubber and his spies closer and closer to the door.

As if by magic, the wind blew itself to the place where the Grubber and his spies stood; the door burst open, a mist filled the corridor, and the Grubber and his spies were blown towards the door, then, the door closed; the mist disappeared taking with it the Grubber and his meldoes.

Jasper and Worminus looked at each other; at last, their enemies had vanished and as they turned towards the creatures which they had helped, a light appeared, shining around the door, and in the light, the face of Armild appeared giving out the message.

"You will always find me in times of trouble, keep the stone safe, continue to defend good from evil." Then, just as quick as the face of Armild had appeared, it disappeared, making Jasper and Worminus know they had started out on a journey to help those in trouble, destroy evil and always go where they would be needed.

The smeldewok wanted to thank their two wonderful friends and as 'Thank you, thank you' rang out, the king stepped forward asking, "How can we repay?"

The two smiled.

"No need to repay, we'll stay."

Knowing they would, till the call came, to start out on:

ANOTHER INCREDIBLE JOURNEY.